Lizzie's Recalcitrant Earl

The Heir and the Spare

Book 3

Fiona Miers

Prologue

1805

The week he turned twenty-one years old, the Honourable Rupert Willoughby packed his bags and bade goodbye to his family. Which also meant farewell to the servants and all the trappings of wealth to which he was accustomed.

The festivities thrown for him had been magnificent and the night with his friends, truly excellent. But now that he had finally reached manhood, there was one more thing for Rupert to do and that was to finally move out of his family home and into bachelor lodgings. His time for drinking the heady wine of freedom and sowing his wild oats had finally arrived.

On his way out the door, he was called into the study by his brother, Henry, who had married the wife chosen for him, and who had inherited the Earldom of Sweeting when their father had passed away a few years earlier.

Rupert knocked on the door and waited, impatiently tapping his feet.

"Please enter," Henry called through the thick, wooden door.

He grinned and took a deep breath. He had no idea what this was going to be about, but hoped it wouldn't take long. His life was calling him, and he didn't want to be late.

He pushed open the door and walked into the opulent, yet tastefully decorated room.

"Good evening, my lord," Rupert said, bowing to his brother before sitting down in the chair opposite.

Rupert had always viewed his brother more like a father than a sibling, Henry being fifteen years his senior. They were brothers and yet they hardly knew each other.

"Firstly, I'd like to congratulate you belatedly on your birthday yesterday. I'm sorry I wasn't there for it," Henry apologised, with what appeared to be honest regret.

"No need, Henry. I know it was essential to be with your wife." Rupert waved his hand dismissively. His brother had been at their country estate whilst his wife was in her confinement. Rupert had known that their fifth child was due any day. They already had four daughters.

"I did, but I am back to speak to you because of what has happened," Henry said, in a rather pompous tone. By Rupert's estimation, there was obviously something serious to report.

"I'm sorry, I don't quite understand. Is everything all right? Mary is not unwell?" Rupert asked, hoping nothing untoward had happened to his sister-in-law. The woman had never been particularly warm toward him, but he didn't wish any ill upon her.

"She gave birth to another girl." Henry groaned, his mouth turning down and his nose wrinkling.

Rupert grimaced internally. He knew that his brother needed an heir, but how many more children could they have?

"Oh...well, congratulations," Rupert said, unable to think of anything else to say.

His brother gave him a rather dry look and placed his hands on the desk in front of him.

"I have no wish to continue to produce daughters. The doctors have told me that more than likely, Mary can only bear female children." His brother hesitated for a moment, then spoke again. "I have a son, after all," he announced, with a victorious smile.

Rupert frowned. He'd known his brother had a long-term mistress, but he hadn't realised that she had borne him a son. Apparently, his brother took this to mean that the continual arrival of daughters couldn't be his fault, as he had sired a son with another woman. Rupert saw the holes in this logic but kept his mouth tightly shut.

"I didn't realise you'd had a child with someone else," Rupert said instead, temporarily blinded to the primary issue his brother was trying to raise.

Again, that smile, a sickening grimace of teeth and lips.

"Yes, with another on the way."

Rupert was struck with a rather frightening realisation. His brother was in love with his mistress.

"But, surely, you will keep trying for an heir with your wife?" he asked quietly, the reality of what his brother was trying to convey slowly sinking into his brain and his heart beginning to pound against his ribs.

"No, I won't be. *You* are my heir."

Rupert's heart sank and his breath caught in his throat. *No, I don't want this.*

"But Henry…" he protested, almost gasping for air as panic began to set in.

"It is settled," Henry announced with finality, holding his hand up to ward off any further rebuttal from Rupert.

"I will increase your allowance as befits your new station," his brother added. "You will have a suitable wife chosen for you in the near future, and she will be the one to produce our heir. It is quite simple. I had thought you would be happy about this."

Rupert could see his life slipping away before it had even begun. He had never wanted this responsibility. He hadn't even decided if he wanted to marry at all.

"But…" Rupert vainly tried to protest once more, a cold sweat breaking out on his brow.

"It is decided." Henry stared him down, his almost black eyes boring into Rupert's.

A familiar stirring in his blood alerted Rupert to a change in his body that he often ignored. He knew he had a temper. By physically abusing his body on a daily basis, he kept it in check with lots of riding, boxing, and rowing. But it was always there, simmering away underneath. His grandfather had the same disposition. He had heard the older servants speak of it. No one except his friends had ever seen the fire unleashed, though. They'd told him bluntly that it wasn't an occurrence they ever wished to see repeated.

Rupert stood up and used what size he had to try and intimidate his brother. He was six feet four inches tall, well over his brother's five feet, eleven inches. He was still lean, but he was developing strength and his shoulders were already considerably wider than Henry's.

"No!" Rupert ground out through clenched teeth, his fingers flexing and extending in shaking movements. "I will not have you choose me a wife to act as your broodmare."

"You will do as you're ordered," his brother shouted, his round face turning a mottled red.

"I will not. If you choose a wife for me who cannot bear sons or any children at all, what will happen to our name?" Rupert argued.

They both knew that a female could inherit the title, in rare circumstances, but a male heir was preferred by all involved.

"You must marry, and soon," his brother said, insistently.

"I will not. I haven't even moved out yet." Rupert almost shouted, clearing his throat in embarrassment as his voice almost broke.

"Then I will cut you off," Henry announced, with a flick of his hand. This was his one and only advantage. He held the power to either make Rupert's life easy and pleasant, or tough indeed.

Rupert frowned at his brother, feeling flames of anger licking their way along his spine.

He held his fists by his side, taking a long, deep breath before he spoke. "Do that, and I'll join the army and disappear. You will never have control over me again, and your precious title can go to the butler for all I care."

He turned toward the door, ready to do exactly what he'd said he would and damn the consequences. He would not be controlled like this.

"Wait," Henry called out, a note of desperation in his voice.

Rupert stopped just before he reached the door, but refused to go back to his brother's desk. Instead, he simply turned and stared at Henry, pouring every ounce of anger into his glare.

"Thirty. Marry by thirty, and I'll make sure you never want for anything," his brother bargained, evidently unwilling to lose his only blood-linked male heir.

Rupert clenched his teeth and used all of his willpower to push back his anger. Slowly, it retreated, like a black cloud into the distance. At last, he could see clearly again.

His brother leaned forward on his desk, no longer in a position of power. He was begging.

Rupert forced his brain to think. Thirty seemed a very long way off. He was barely one and twenty. Nine years he had. Nine years to sow his wild oats. Nine years to drink enough liquor to kill a sailor. He had nine years of sweet freedom before he finally sold his soul to his brother for the sake of money.

After a few moments, he nodded. "Done."

The decision was final.

Chapter 1

London 1813

Rupert Willoughby was strikingly handsome. Or so he'd been told, for as long as he could remember. The combination of truly blue eyes and black hair had enticed many a beauty into his bed.

Thanks to his brother's wealth and generosity, he had an excellent allowance. Rupert's best friend, the former Lord Archibald Turner, now the Earl of Tother, an original member of their group, "the spares," was a dab hand at the Stock Exchange. Archie often advised Rupert about how to invest his money and thus, he was set for the future. Rupert would never have to seek employment as so many second sons had to do.

He secretly wanted a wife such as his friends Archie, and Oliver, Duke of Lincoln, had found. Sarah, Duchess of Lincoln, and Charlotte, Countess of Tother, were both ladies who could hold an intelligent conversation and also manage a household. Both were beautiful, and much more than merely decorative. Rupert wasn't sure if he would ever find such a woman for himself and certainly not one who could hold his interest in the bedchamber. It would probably be better to find a 'suitable" wife and continue to live as he already did. As long as he produced the required heir, his responsibilities to his brother and the family would be met.

At the Duke and Duchess of Lincoln's annual ball, Rupert eyed the beauty talking to the Countess of Tother. The former Lady Charlotte Dunford looked very well, beautiful, in fact. She was still quite blissfully happy with her marriage to Archie, and if Rupert wasn't mistaken, could very well have been *enceinte* again. Unlike many of the women of the *ton* who all but hid throughout their pregnancies, Charlotte glowed with good health and happily stood in the centre of a crowded ballroom. She had no qualms showing everyone how happy she was to be bearing another child for her husband. Rupert shook his head against the unfamiliar notion. It was confounding.

Next to her, however, was a young lady whom Rupert had never seen before. She had hair as blonde as Sarah's. She had tan skin in comparison to Charlotte's paleness, but the colour suited her hair. He couldn't see her eyes very well from where he was standing, but it appeared to him that they looked quite dark. She was striking. She had high cheekbones, classic features, and an amazing smile that affected him even from where he was standing, right across the room. Rarely had Rupert seen a more beautiful woman.

She was short in stature and had high, firm breasts, swelling above her low neckline. The blue of her dress and her wedding ring proclaimed her married. Or widowed, perhaps. Either way, she was the perfect rendezvous he needed. He was a little bored with his latest mistress.

Rupert adjusted his coat with a quick tug and straightened to his full height. Feeling confident, he walked over to the two ladies.

"May I beg you for an introduction to your friend, my dear Charlotte?"

Charlotte smiled tightly, knowing his habits well. She turned to include him in their circle, which surprised him a little, but his friend's sister did have perfect manners.

"Of course, Rupert. Mrs. Elizabeth Symmons, may I introduce a friend of ours, the Honourable Rupert Willoughby, the younger brother of the Earl of Sweeting."

Rupert heard the warning in the introduction and smirked inwardly. Charlotte was fiercely protectively of those she loved. It was one of the things he liked most about her.

The beautiful blonde curtseyed prettily and gave him a sunny, open smile. Rupert bowed in return, surprised by the artlessness of her expression.

"May I have the pleasure of the next dance, my lady?" he asked, giving her his most charming smile.

Elizabeth smiled back, glancing quickly at Charlotte for permission to leave her alone, which Rupert respected. When Charlotte smiled back in return, the beautiful woman turned to him.

"Of course. Thank you, sir," she replied confidently, placing her small hand in his.

She was petite, yet Rupert felt the firmness of her grip and observed the way she held herself. This would not be a woman over whom one could easily walk, he realised.

"You are looking charming this evening, Mrs. Symmons," Rupert told her, as they swept onto the dance floor.

Elizabeth laughed, her bright eyes sparkling with gaiety.

"Why, thank you, sir. And indeed, you are looking very handsome."

Rupert grinned, surprised by her words. He didn't believe he had ever had a compliment returned before. Most women only fluttered their fans and gave him the eyes. The eyes told him how flattered they were that he had given them his attention. The eyes also indicated to him just how quickly they would fall into his bed. Mrs. Elizabeth Symmons wasn't giving him the eyes, nor was she flirting with him. How strange. She was difficult to read.

"How are you enjoying the evening?" Rupert asked politely, maneuvering her expertly around the many couples on the dance floor. He didn't dance often, but he considered it part of his seduction routine and therefore made sure that he was rather good at it.

"Oh, I am enjoying it very much. I have recently come out of mourning and have never felt so decadent for wearing a colour before." Elizabeth looked down for a moment on her beautiful blue evening gown.

Rupert smiled inwardly. A widow, was she? That was perfect. Affairs were much less stressful when there wasn't a spouse to take into consideration all the time. Would Elizabeth Symmons like just a night or two in his arms? Or would she perhaps want something more permanent? A longer time frame would work out quite nicely, Rupert thought, his mind jumping ahead with plans for her seduction.

"You must be lonely," Rupert murmured, giving her a look that was meant to be both respectful, yet meaningful to those who knew how to interpret it.

He swept his eyes subtly down to her neckline, where there was a swelling of flesh. He shifted his stance slightly, as his cock thickened in his breeches. He was surprised, but also delighted. He hadn't experienced such a strong attraction to a woman in a very long time. His body was alive, all but screaming out to lay her down on the nearest flat surface and have his wicked way with her.

His body and mind declared war. It was his primitive self, versus the cultured *ton* gentleman. If he were truly honest with himself, he had been bored for quite some time. Nothing was ever new or exciting anymore, but he had a feeling that this woman would be different.

"Indeed I am, my lord."

* * *

Lizzie looked up at Rupert's handsome face, seeing him with fresh eyes. Was this gentleman in the market for a wife? He looked a few years older than her, but that was never a good indication of the intention to settle down. A man could be five and twenty, or five and forty and still be an eligible match. Unlike a woman, who had certain limitations, this handsome man in front of her did not. Lizzie inhaled discreetly and noted that he didn't smell of too much alcohol. His clothes were tailored rather beautifully. He either had independent means, or he was searching for an heiress and had spent every penny on looking delicious. Lizzie couldn't tell which. She would have to ask Charlotte for more information about this gentleman. But Lizzie could tell that the man in front of her was confident, almost arrogant, in his countenance.

She looked up again and caught her breath when Rupert met her gaze. Something new and unusual stirred in her belly whenever she looked into his rather remarkable black eyes. The feeling wasn't altogether pleasant, but at the same time, it was exciting. He was the first gentleman to spark any interest in her since the death of her husband.

"Perhaps you would permit me to escort you home tonight?" Rupert suggested, his eyes now taking on a strange sort of leer. He couldn't mean what she thought, surely?

"I don't think so." She frowned. He couldn't be serious, could he? Her mind was racing. Was he suggesting that she take him home and...bed him?

Something in his gaze hinted that was exactly what he wanted.

Any ideas she had of him as a potential husband ended right there. She mentally catalogued him as a rake and by definition, not interested in marriage. She wiped the smile from her face and straightened. She was almost a foot shorter than he was, but anger began to build in her belly, lending her an extra inch or so of height in her straightened spine.

"I can be very persuasive, ma'am," Rupert whispered, his voice laced with honey and giving her a grin which, she was sure, had won many a woman before her.

She snorted, glaring up at the man she had momentarily considered as a prospective husband and now viewed as a big oaf.

"You can be as persuasive as you like, sir, but I am not in the least interested in a dalliance."

"I can assure you, I will make it a pleasurable interlude." Rupert drew Lizzie away from the main body of dancers so that they were on the edge of the dance floor. At least he had pitched his voice low.

Again, he flashed that dazzling smile and Lizzie frowned. Rupert Willoughby hadn't been denied before, that was plain to see. His thumb gently stroked her hand and that strange flutter moved low in her belly, again. It was time to nip this in the bud.

"I want a husband, sir, and children, not an interlude, however pleasurable. Can you give me what I want?" Lizzie batted her eyelashes and injected honey into her own tone. She knew the last thing this charming rakehell of a gentleman would want was to be shackled forever to one woman. The best way of making him stay away from her was to be honest about what she wanted from this year's London season.

Rupert's eyes widened, and as they continued their dance. he tripped and stumbled a little. Lizzie gripped his hand and waited for him to regain his composure, trying not to laugh.

"Uh, no," Rupert answered, his calm facade wavering completely now.

Lizzie watched the play of strange emotions run across Rupert's face and wanted to smooth his furrowed brow with her fingers. This thought was shocking enough to pull her out of her daze, and she snapped out the first thing that came into her mind.

"Then, you will never get me into your bed. I suggest that you take home the woman in green who has been eyeing you for the past hour, and leave me alone."

Damn! She hadn't meant to be so obvious in her jealousy. She dropped her hands from Rupert's, turned and stormed away.

* * *

Rupert watched her go, feeling something akin to complete shock. He had never been denied before and had never had to fight for something he wanted, as friends of his had had to do. Ladies clamoured for his company in bed. He had never had to try too hard before. Rupert wanted them, and they gave him everything they had. It had always been very simple.

Rupert discreetly looked in the direction Lizzie had indicated. There was, indeed, a beautiful woman in a green gown giving him looks that could only be described as desirous. That was the norm.

He would get an introduction to her, take her for a walk or a dance, and within a few moments, she would be in a carriage on her way home to meet him. If, of course, she hadn't decided that the study would be easier.

He took another look.

The woman in green seemed like a "can't wait until we get home, let's go to the study" type lady. Rupert felt no urge to go up and speak to her, no call to tup her, nothing. It was like his libido had departed when the woman with whom he had been dancing did. Most unusual.

He turned and noticed Mrs. Elizabeth Symmons chatting again with Charlotte. Rupert watched as Charlotte threw back her head and even heard her laugh from where he was standing. He couldn't stop the flush that spread across his cheeks. Were they laughing at him?

Turning on his heel, he headed straight to the card room to drown his disappointment in a brandy.

Chapter 2

Lizzie watched Rupert walk toward the card room and couldn't suppress her triumphant grin. Charlotte, Countess of Tother, had laughed loud enough to be heard clear across the ballroom. That would teach him not to be such a cad. Despicable!

"I can't believe he had the gall to proposition me so," Lizzie exclaimed to her friend, huffing in exasperation. Why would he have propositioned her? Did she appear to be a lady who would be easily enticed by a handsome face?

Charlotte giggled again, a milder version of her previous laugh, but still, a show of genuine amusement.

"What I can't believe is that someone has turned him down.

That would have to be a first for Rupert." Charlotte chuckled again, loudly, fluttering her fan to try and cover some of the noise.

"What do you mean? Why would a woman indulge in that sort of activity outside of marriage? It's not as though it's even pleasant." Lizzie shook her head.

She looked up and noticed Charlotte blushing crimson. The unshakeable countess never blushed, so Lizzie was quite confident she must have said something terribly wrong and obviously inappropriate. Oh, she could be so common sometimes!

"Oh, dearest Lady Charlotte, please forgive me for saying such a thing in your company. You are obviously not accustomed to such a common expression." Lizzie apologised profusely. Having spent a year as an army wife, such speech was now commonplace to her. How could she have forgotten where and with whom she was conversing?

The countess burst out laughing afresh, even louder than she had when Lizzie told her what Rupert had wanted from her. Now it was Lizzie's turn to heat with embarrassment and confusion. Charlotte suddenly seemed to notice the curious looks they were receiving, thanks to her rather unladylike outbursts.

"Shall we stroll along the patio?" Charlotte suggested invitingly, linking her arm with the other woman's and turning them both toward the doors before Lizzie could even reply.

"Of course," Lizzie murmured, happy for an opportunity to go out into the fresh air. She had forgotten just how stuffy London ballrooms could be. She missed the countryside immensely. As they stepped onto the balcony, Charlotte led Lizzie to an unoccupied corner and turned her around, so they were face to face.

"I'm sorry Lizzie, I shouldn't have laughed. You didn't shock me at all with your words," Charlotte explained, whispering in a conspiratorial sort of way.

"Really? Then why did you blush so brightly?" Lizzie asked, confused now.

Charlotte flushed rather prettily again, and Lizzie wanted to bite her tongue. Why was she saying everything that came into her head? When would she learn to control her words?

"Because you said that there was no pleasure in the bedchamber," Charlotte explained, with a rather guilty smile.

Lizzie eyed her friend critically. Surely Charlotte wasn't suggesting what Lizzie thought she was? "Well, there wasn't for me…not that it was unpleasant all of the time," she hastened to add, feeling that she was being disrespectful toward her late husband with her words. He had tried to be gentle with her and had never deliberately hurt her, unlike some of the husbands in the stories she had heard. The marriage bed had never been something to which she'd looked forward, but, in fairness, she'd never dreaded it either.

Charlotte seemed to be battling with what to say next. She wasn't speaking, and yet her eyes were telling Lizzie just how much she disagreed with Lizzie's opinion on matters of the bedchamber.

"You enjoy it?" Lizzie squeaked, not sure if she could believe what she was reading in Charlotte's face. How was it possible?

"Yes, I do," Charlotte admitted, apparently battling another urge to laugh. The corners of her mouth kept lifting up, as though they had a mind of their own.

"Oh." Lizzie sighed. She had heard that some women did. Thinking back, there had been moments with her husband that had been pleasant. He had kissed her occasionally, or touched her in ways that had given her pleasure. It was just the bedding that had been uncomfortable. Perhaps there were men who could make that part pleasurable too? It seemed unlikely, but she supposed it was possible.

"Really?" Lizzie asked again, her eyes opening wide. She searched Charlotte's face for any sign that she wasn't serious.

This time Charlotte lost the control over her laughter and giggled openly.

"Archie is a little different from most men and my marriage is a love match. I think that helps," Charlotte explained, with a smile that showed how much she was hiding in that statement.

Lizzie pondered this. Her marriage had been a love match too. Well, perhaps not exactly, but it hadn't been about dowries and connections. Perhaps if there were more affection in her next marriage, there would be more pleasure?

Either way, she wasn't risking becoming pregnant or ruining her reputation for the sake of finding out from the Honourable Rupert Willoughby.

"Perhaps my next husband will make it more pleasurable. But all I want is a home and children," Lizzie announced, unfazed by this turn of events.

In her experience, her husband would come to her bed three or four times a month, and leave after about ten minutes. It would be a small price to pay for a child if she managed to conceive in her next marriage.

Charlotte simply nodded, but Lizzie could tell she wanted to say more.

"Well, if you ever find that you need to talk to someone about it, let me know," she offered with a kind smile.

Lizzie thought that very unlikely but thanked her all the same.

She was twenty-five years old and had been born late in life to her parents, who had loved each other very much. Both parents came from good families. Her father was the son of an earl, and her mother was the daughter of the younger brother of a duke. Her father had been an academic and her mother, after marriage, had discovered that she had a talent for languages.

Lizzie had never wanted for anything. She had made a good match at twenty-three with the second son of a viscount who had a commission in the army. He had been a kind husband, but he drank a little too often and had sometimes gambled too much. Lizzie had some income from her parents, and she had often had to resort to using her money to pay for essentials when her husband had been too frivolous. Lizzie didn't mind too much about that. She didn't need fancy gowns and trips away. But after less than twelve months, her husband had died from a fever. Lizzie had been left a childless widow at the age of twenty-four.

Now, she was back in London. She had been given a small townhouse by her mother, who believed that a lady should always be independent, if possible. Lizzie also had a small income from both her husband's family as well as her own. She had no need to marry a man with deep pockets, yet she didn't want a fortune hunter who would marry her for her money, either. Lizzie hadn't told anyone of her situation, and she hoped it wouldn't become necessary to do so. She wanted a good husband who wanted to look after her, not one whom she would have to look after instead.

Lizzie knew exactly what she wanted in a husband. She wanted a man who preferred the country to town and didn't gamble or drink to excess. A man who wanted children and didn't wish to have them banished to the nursery the moment they were born. She wanted a large family after growing up as an only child, and she wanted a father for her children such as she had once had. A man who was interested in her and their children the way her father had been interested in her and her mother.

Thanks to her loving and attentive parents, Lizzie had been

brought up in good society and had never been submitted to the neglect and abuse that many other children had been–or suffered. She also wanted a man who would be faithful, however unusual that seemed to be in a *ton* marriage. She was hopeful she would manage to find such a match if she tried.

Being a widow meant that she had fewer rules to contend with than the virgins flitting around the ballrooms. That didn't mean, in any way, that she wanted to sample the men before choosing one, but it just meant that she could go for walks and have private talks without being forced to marry, as she would have, had she been an unmarried lady.

She had spoken the truth to Charlotte. Lizzie didn't enjoy the bedding part of marriage, but she understood that it was necessary for procreation. And it wasn't horrible, just a little uncomfortable. She had to admit that part of her had enjoyed the comfort and pleasure her husband had taken in her body. Regardless, no matter how she felt about it, she was determined to marry again. Lizzie wanted nothing except to have a comfortable life with a husband and children by her side. No rake, no matter how handsome, was going to tempt her to change her mind.

Chapter 3

Rupert visited Archie and Charlotte, the Earl and Countess of Tother, the next day. As Archie was with his solicitor, so the butler informed, Rupert was shown into the sitting room where Charlotte sat embroidering as he entered. She placed her needlework aside as soon as she saw him and smiled from her comfortable place on the chaise.

Rupert had often found it amusing to tease Charlotte, once she was married to his friend. She knew him well enough to know that he mostly bedded bored, married ladies. So, he played on that with her, touching her arm or shoulder, just to see her reaction. He would never betray Archie in such a way, of course, but Rupert still liked to tease. Charlotte always blushed furiously and swatted him away. She never looked scared or he wouldn't have continued, she just looked wholly uninterested in what he was suggesting.

He admired her loyalty.

However, Charlotte was pregnant again and that meant no teasing. Rupert had never bedded a woman who was *enceinte* and never intended to do so. Once his future wife had conceived, he could see himself staying out of her chamber for the foreseeable future. There were always plenty of available women for him. He needn't bother his wife.

Looking at the healthy glow of Charlotte's cheeks, though, Rupert knew that Archie didn't feel the same way.

"How does it feel to find a woman who doesn't want you?" Charlotte asked with a cheeky grin and a hand straying to her softly rounded belly.

Rupert's eyes locked onto her hand. He couldn't drag his gaze away from the picture of Charlotte gently caressing herself. The thought made him blush, despite his conscious effort not to respond in any obvious way. Rupert knew he should be listening to the words Charlotte was saying, but he couldn't ignore what she was doing.

Archie was lucky to have such a sensual wife.

Charlotte stood up with a smug grin plastered on her face and advanced on Rupert.

"Would you like to feel the baby, Rupert?" Charlotte asked, moving closer to where he was sitting and reaching out to grab hold of one of his hands.

"No, thank you." Rupert almost shouted, moving away from her as fast as he could. He was shocked and terrified that she would suggest such a thing. A lady was meant to disguise herself when she was with child, not call attention to it. How dare she ask him to *touch* it?

"The baby has just started to move. It is really quite amazing," she smiled as she backed him into a corner of the sitting room. Charlotte's dress swished softly as she moved and Rupert realised he had never heard such a scary noise before. His heart was pounding wildly behind his black vest. She was getting closer and he was trapped.

"No, Charlotte, please." Rupert was all but yelling now, panic setting in as his shoulders hit a wall. How had he backed himself into a corner?

Charlotte reached out to him and grabbed both of his hands. Her own hands were soft and warm to the touch and Rupert instinctively relaxed. Her touch was oddly reassuring and he forgot to fight her.

Charlotte brought his resisting hands up, and because he wouldn't allow her to bring them closer to her belly, she brought her belly to him. It was shocking to Rupert that he almost had her stomach and breasts touching his jacket, because she was only scant inches from that feat. He had never been so close to a woman he wasn't in the act of seducing.

Rupert was trapped, by both his curiosity and by this woman whom he had known for fifteen years. It wasn't proper. She was married to one of his friends and yet there was some sort of perverse desire to know what it felt like to hold a child still growing in its mother's womb.

Without any further preparation, his hands were on either side of her round, hard abdomen. Rupert sucked in a lungful of air and tried to drag his eyes away from the incredible image of his hands cupping Charlotte's growing babe. His hands instinctively moulded to the shape and he felt the warmth of her through her dress.

There was a small flutter of movement and then a strong push against Rupert's right hand. At that exact moment, something inside Rupert shifted irrevocably and his heart melted a little.

That strange pull that he had been feeling ever since his friends had married women they loved seemed to increase in strength. Fear made Rupert's breath whistle through his throat. How was he going to survive such a situation?

"I see you finally got your hands on my wife," Archie's drawl came from the direction of the door.

Rupert pulled his hands away so quickly he couldn't have looked more guilty. He tried to take a step back and away from the beautiful woman who he had been touching and realised he was already pressed up against the wall.

"I'm sorry, Archie, I didn't mean to..." Rupert hurried to apologise, his cheeks flushing with an intense heat.

Archie put out his hand and beckoned his cheeky wife, who promptly returned to his side with a satisfied smile on her face.

"Have you been harassing my friend, Charlotte?" Archie asked his wife with a teasing grin as he wrapped an arm around her swollen waistline.

Charlotte rubbed her belly again as she leaned into his embrace.

"Not at all, my lord. I thought I would introduce Rupert to the next member of our family. After all, he would make an excellent godparent."

Rupert exhaled sharply. Had he been kicked in the chest?

He had never been asked to be a godparent to any of his sister's children, nor even one of his brother's five daughters. They had always expressed their belief that he was too irresponsible. It had hurt every time they had chosen others, although he never said so.

Rupert swallowed against the rather embarrassing urge to

shed tears of emotion and noticed Archie watching him with those keen, hawk eyes that never missed anything.

"You're supposed to ask Rupert if he would like to be our next child's godfather, not just announce your intent, Charlotte." Archie chided good-naturedly, directing his wife back to a chair.

Charlotte dropped into the armchair with more grace than a woman of her size should be able to muster. Raised by a formidable duchess, Charlotte was a lady in every sense of the word—her liking of her husband's marriage bed notwithstanding.

"Why? We weren't asked to be David's godparents. It was just announced at the christening," she answered, giving her husband a playful swat with her hand.

They both turned and looked at Rupert expectantly. Was he meant to act as though it had been a request?

"I would be honoured," Rupert answered gruffly. Unable to say anything else, he bowed in thanks. How could he be getting so emotional over such a thing? He really was changing. It was a sobering thought and he cringed.

"See?" Charlotte smiled happily at her husband and thanked the maid who had brought in tea, cakes and whiskey.

Rupert saw the alcohol and knew it had been brought in on a tea tray for him. Archie hardly ever drank hard spirits, and never this early in the day. Obviously, the butler knew him well. The thought saddened him a little. When had he become predictable? Boring, even?

"Whiskey or tea?" Charlotte asked him politely, already reaching for the whiskey bottle.

"Tea please," Rupert responded before he could stop himself.

After Charlotte's earlier assault on his person he really needed a whiskey, but was sick of being the man everyone expected him to be.

Charlotte's eyebrows shot up, but she didn't say anything

except to ask, "How do you take it?" . She poured the tea into three cups.

"Milk and two sugars please," he told her with confidence. When was the last time he had actually drunk tea? He couldn't remember, but decided to brazen it out and sat down gratefully into a chair opposite her. Archie sat also, in the chair closest to his wife. He reached for a cake and absently touched Charlotte on the back of the neck.

Rupert watched Charlotte lean into the caress like a flower facing the sun. It only took that one small gesture and Rupert had to look away from his friends. He had never wanted Charlotte; never thought of her that way. But sometimes Rupert wished he could find what his friends had found. A woman who had the qualities of both a wife and a mistress. Someone who would keep his home running, make him laugh, attend to his children, join him in social outings *and* happily join him in his bed. Charlotte was pregnant for the second time in twelve months and Sarah had just given birth to her second son in less than two years. There was much bedding going on and his friend's wives obviously enjoyed it. Sarah had even said as much the year before. Rupert coughed at the memory.

"Have you seen Sarah and Oliver's new son yet?" Charlotte asked him as she bit into one of the cakes on the tray.

Rupert looked up from his beverage. Sometimes he wondered if Charlotte was a mind reader. How could she have known he had been thinking about such things?

"Yes, last week. He looks just like Oliver," Rupert said, to no one in particular. He had been surprised when he had received a summons to meet the new Lincoln baby. He had never seen a baby who was only a few weeks old before.

Sarah, however, being a vicar's daughter, had been anxious

to have the baby christened at the earliest opportunity, and this time it had been a small, family affair.

Even his nieces had been kept away from everyone until they were several months old. It had been amazing. The infant had been rather cross looking, red and wrinkled, but miraculous in its perfection as a tiny human being. Rupert would never say this out loud, but the experience had actually made him yearn for a son himself.

Charlotte chuckled loudly.

"Well, who else would he look like?" she asked, smiling as though it would be unusual for a cuckoo to be born into a nest of the *ton*. Hah!

Rupert stared at Charlotte a moment longer and could barely believe this was the same woman who had once proclaimed she would never marry because a husband would have access to her body. Rupert marvelled at how incredible it was that things could change when someone met the right person.

"True. His wife is Sarah, after all," said Rupert. His implication was that any other lady of the *ton* might have been having an affair, having provided her husband with an heir, but certainly not Sarah, with her impeccable reputation for loyalty. Rupert knew it in his bones.

Charlotte and Archie gave each other a puzzled look.

"No witty rejoinder about the average married lady of the *ton*?" Archie asked, giving him a quizzical look.

Rupert shook his head. What could he say? How could he joke about arranged marriages and faithless women when Sarah and Charlotte were now his examples and the wives of his closest friends? It would dishonour all of them, not to mention the fact that he didn't lie well.

"That's only because of Lizzie," Charlotte scoffed, giving her husband a knowing look. "Rupert finally found a widow who didn't jump directly into bed with him at the first opportunity."

Rupert gripped the tiny teacup tightly, setting it down after a moment lest he break it. It was Charlotte's intention to get a rise out of him of course, but he still fought the anger, unwilling to let her win.

"I haven't given up on that widow. She just needs to get to know me better," Rupert declared, with all the arrogance he possessed. And considering his appearance and breeding, that conceit was considerable. So, it was quite a blow to his pride when Archie and Charlotte both laughed.

"Well, you have charmed more women that I can count, Rupert. I'm sure it won't be that difficult," Archie said quietly, taking a sip of his tea.

Rupert smiled indulgently, Archie had heard about his conquests so frequently that when it came to his wedding night, the virginal Archie had come to him for advice. Rupert had never admitted it, but he had taken that fact as a huge compliment.

"You both are so wrong. If you think Lizzie is just like every other bored matron, then you are in for a surprise." Charlotte smiled smugly and bit into a sugary shortbread.

"How is she so different?" Rupert asked, succumbing to the delicious looking sweets in front of him. Biting into an apple cake, he almost groaned in pleasure. He really needed to invest in a better chef at his own home.

Elizabeth Symmons may have said no to him once, but how long could that last? For how long could she hold off? He had never really pursued a woman before, but it couldn't be very different from a normal conquest. He would just savour it more when he finally won her.

"You mean, apart from the fact that she is present during the Season this year for the sole purpose of remarriage?"

"Well, that doesn't mean she can't dally with me," Rupert argued, setting his jaw.

What would be the problem with that? It had happened to Rupert before. He would bed a widow who would try to trap him into marriage, only to find him immovable on the subject. The widow would then move on and marry the next suitable gentleman soon after and he, too, would be onto the next available lady. That was the best thing about bedding widows and married women. He couldn't be forced to marry any of them.

"Why would she waste her time?" Charlotte asked him with a straight face. Well, as straight a face as Charlotte could pull, considering that her eyes were laughing. She never could hide her feelings very well and Rupert frowned at what she wasn't saying.

"Charlotte, coming from you, isn't that a bit hypocritical?" He was fed up with being fodder for this couple's amusement. If there was one thing he deplored, it was hypocrisy and here was a woman who had married because she was pregnant!

"What do you mean by that?" Charlotte asked, flushing with discomfort at the obvious implication.

Rupert, seeing the danger, ignored Archie's angry glare and answered regardless.

"I mean that if a lady like you can indulge before marriage, why wouldn't your Lizzie?"

Charlotte jumped to her feet and Archie followed just as quickly, placing his hand in the small of her back to steady her. Rupert followed suit, his anger still rising. Archie put his other hand out to calm her, but she shook it off.

"The difference is love, Rupert, which you wouldn't understand. I have loved Archie for a long time and our actions were because of that fact. Not for any other reason. Until you learn about love, you will never have the privilege of knowing a woman like Elizabeth Symmons!"

Charlotte turned on her heel and walked straight out of the room.

A moment of silence went by and then he heard his friend's heavy sigh.

"You shouldn't have said that, Rupert."

Archie hadn't moved since Charlotte had left the room, but Rupert could see how hard he was fighting to remain still.

"I should go," Rupert announced, feeling foolish. Why did he let his temper get the better of him? Charlotte had only been joking. Did it really bother him *that* much that he had missed out on a frolic with her friend? *Surely not?*

"You will not. You just insulted my wife, who is in a delicate condition, and for whom I know you care a great deal. Now you and I will have a talk and I want you to tell me what the hell is going on."

Rupert regarded his stoic and gentle friend in astonishment. He had never heard Archie use such language before.

"Please accept my apologies. I am very sorry indeed for speaking indiscreetly to Lady Charlotte ...um...the countess." Rupert spoke stiffly. Unaccustomed as he was to apologising, this pricked his pride considerably.

"So, you should be," Archie retorted, his arms now calmly tucked behind his back. Rupert wasn't fooled for a moment. There was a fire still blazing in Archie's eyes.

His friend continued to look at him expectantly and Rupert sighed. What could he say? That he was jealous of his friend's marriage? Never! He would rather be thrown out of a carriage at high speed than admit that.

"I simply let my temper get the better of me, Archie. The

truth is, I find her teasing goes slightly too far at times. But I accept that I shouldn't have said anything."

"You're not telling me the truth, Rupert."

He sighed loudly. Damned if he'd tell Archie the truth. A thought came to him and his mood lightened.

"I'm bored with my latest mistress and I'm a bit frustrated. I'm not accustomed to abstinence, old friend." Rupert grinned devilishly at Archie, who up until a couple of years ago, had been a virgin.

Archie just stared at him with his cold, assessing, brown eyes and said nothing. Rupert swallowed uncomfortably, wondering what his friend could see. Was his loneliness so obvious?

"Did you get my letter about the latest investment that I think you should place money in?" Archie asked, changing the subject for reasons unknown.

Rupert sighed inwardly, grateful that his friend had obviously chosen to show mercy.

Rupert stayed for another half hour, talking to Archie about his latest tips and trading advice, before making his excuses and leaving. Archie had even recommended a new horse breeder with foals for sale from a bloodline that Rupert had been wanting to buy into for years. However, none of this mundane talk distracted Rupert completely from his confusion. That night, a bottle of whiskey did. At least for a few hours.

Chapter 4

Lizzie missed the countryside. It was her home, the place she was happiest and most comfortable. London suffocated her. She had an urgent need to get out into the fresh air, so she put on her prettiest walking dress, picked up her matching parasol and strode down the front steps of her house, thanking the lord that, as a widow, she did not need to wait for an escort.

It was a short walk to the nearby park and she desperately needed to see something other than cobblestone roads, the inside of a carriage or yet another ballroom.

Ten minutes later she was strolling beneath beautiful oak trees, lost in her own little world. She vaguely sensed someone behind her and moved to the left of the path, so the other party could pass if they wanted to do so. Lizzie was feeling peaceful and didn't bother to look and see who was following so closely behind.

"Mrs. Symmons?" Lizzie was astonished to hear Rupert's voice. She whirled and there he was in front of her. He greeted her with a bow.

Lizzie stared around, unable to decide exactly what to do. Random thoughts whirled through her head.

Where did he come from?

He's alone. I am alone.

Has he planned this, somehow?

He can't really be here for me, can he?

"The Honourable Mr. Willoughby. Good day," she returned, finally curtseying.

"Please, call me Rupert." he invited her, seemingly out of breath. Had he rushed to catch her up? "I really don't like my last name," he added with a charming smile.

"Oh, I couldn't possibly," Lizzie exclaimed, surprised by his forwardness.

She had never had a gentleman pursue her with such dishonourable intentions before. It was quite disconcerting how effective he was at the task. Lizzie's heart beat twice as quickly as it should have and her body tightened in all sorts of unusual places.

She began to walk along the path again, faster than before. Rupert trailed at her heels.

"Why ever not? Charlotte does," he pointed out amiably, pulling up beside her and easily matching her fast pace with his long legs.

Lizzie slowed and let him walk beside her. Charlotte did call him by his first name, but she had known the man for most of her life. Also, Rupert wasn't trying to get Charlotte into bed.

"The countess has known you for many years. But I have not. No, I don't think so," Lizzie said gently, twirling her parasol and watching as two children raced across the park ahead of their governess. Such a beautiful scene, one for which she wished so desperately.

"For how long were you married, Mrs. Symmons, before your husband's untimely demise?" Rupert asked, his question taking her by surprise.

"Eleven months," Lizzie replied, still watching the children. The scene before her was such a wonderful sight, but for her, it was like a double-edged sword. She loved to see children, happy and healthy, running about, but doing that left a hollow feeling in her belly. Would she ever have children of her own?

"And you were happy?"

"Yes and no," Lizzie answered honestly. She had decided that being herself as much as possible was the best way to handle this rather intimidating gentleman. He would soon back off from his pursuit of her when he realised what sort of lady she was. Surely, he would soon turn his quest to a more willing female. The thought saddened her a little and Lizzie focused her mind back on the question he had asked.

"We had a good marriage as far as most modern marriages are measured. But he was a little too wild. He was always gambling and drinking with his army friends," Lizzie explained, looking directly into Rupert's eyes for the first time since he had happened upon her.

My goodness, but he was handsome.

"Ah," Rupert nodded, and then made a hand gesture that encouraged her to continue talking.

"When I marry the next time, I really need a gentleman who

will be happy to spend more nights at home with me. I want a man who likes children, and who wants an active role in their lives," she explained, not sure why she was revealing such information to a man who had so casually propositioned her.

Perhaps that was why. So that he would know for sure that she wasn't the right one for him to pursue.

Lizzie began walking again, then stopped, wanting to look at Rupert one more time. It was completely unfair that he was so incredibly handsome.

Rupert gave her a charismatic smile and then laughed. The sound was musical, with the headiness of sweet sherry about it.

"There aren't a lot of men who actively want to play a part in their children's upbringing, Mrs. Symmons. My father certainly didn't in our case, and my brother doesn't with his children."

He grimaced and she wondered what had caused such displeasure. Squashing the urge to contain her curiosity, as any well-bred lady should, she asked him straight out.

"What were you thinking about, just then?" She pointed her finger at his face in one of the most unladylike gestures she had ever dared make.

As quick as a flash, his look disappeared and a haughtiness reserved for the *ton*'s elite appeared in its place. Lizzie wanted to pound the man on his oversized chest.

"Nothing of consequence," Rupert said, in an obvious lie. She stared at him a moment longer before calling him on the untruth.

"Liar," she pronounced, and with a flip of her hand to dismiss him, continued walking.

* * *

Rupert stood still for a full ten seconds, frozen in shock. No one had ever had the gall to say such a thing to him and no woman had ever walked away from him before. *Ridiculous situation!*

It took him several moments to catch up with her even with his considerably longer legs. He knew he should be furious that she had said such a thing to him, but the problem was that it was true and, therefore, he had no grounds to be angry with her.

They ambled along at a slower pace, until Lizzie stopped at a park bench and sat down. Staring around at the view, she sighed with what appeared to be happiness.

Rupert watched her uneasily. He was being ignored and he did not like the feeling. He had never been ignored by a woman, not once in his life. Lizzie seemed as happy and relaxed as though he weren't standing over her, all six feet, four inches of him.

He cleared his throat audibly, but she didn't respond.

Rupert set his jaw against the anger settling in. He considered walking off and leaving her alone, but that wouldn't suit his purpose.

"Elizabeth," he growled, unable to bear being ignored a moment longer. How humiliating, and him the *ton's* most popular rake.

Lizzie's eyes snapped to him at last.

"I did not give you leave to use my Christian name," she said, fire flickering in her usually warm brown eyes.

Rupert grinned, ecstatic to have elicited a reaction. He felt like a five-year-old but at least he finally had her attention.

"You were ignoring me," he said, giving her his most charming smile and crossing his arms across his chest. He hoped the action would highlight his manly chest and muscled arms.

She glared at him.

"Of course, I was. If you don't want to have a proper

conversation with me, you may as well leave," she snapped again, waving her hand toward the edge of the park.

Rupert's smile fell off his face as quickly as it had appeared. What was she talking about?

"Of course, I want to have a proper conversation with you," he argued, confused now. When had he given her the impression he *didn't* want to talk to her?

"Then why did you lie to me?"

Rupert opened his mouth to deny her claim, then shut it again with a snap. She wasn't the usual *ton* lady. He couldn't charm his way out of this. Fear prickled on his skin as he chose to do something he rarely did with anyone, even his friends. His senses told him to run, but instead he moved to the other end of the park bench and sat, turning to face her.

"I have never shared my thoughts with anyone," he admitted, guarded despite his best intentions to remain charming. It had been a long time since he'd been completely honest with anyone and it was difficult.

Lizzie's shoulders seemed to sag as if with relief.

"Then say that, but don't lie to me. You asked me a question and I told you the truth. I expect the same in return. I am not someone who tolerates lying and I'm not someone you are going to charm into your bed. Stop trying so hard. I like you much better this way," she stated, then flushed as Rupert's eyebrows shot up.

One of the most genuine smiles of Rupert's life spread across his face. *She likes me now, does she?*

Lizzie held up her hand. "Don't start feeling pompous about that. I'm not sure you can manage to be honest for more than one sentence."

The barb hit somewhere near Rupert's heart and he shifted

uncomfortably. Why did he have a sudden and rather intense urge to pull her into him for a kiss?

What insanity is this? They were in the middle of a very public area. She would be ruined. Hell, *he* would be ruined. Forever!

"I was thinking about my brother," Rupert explained gruffly, before he lost the nerve. The words stuck in his throat. He coughed loudly and swallowed.

Lizzie smiled encouragingly.

"He has five daughters and doesn't intend to have any more children with his wife. Therefore, I am his only male heir."

"Does he have other children?" she asked softly, seeming to realise what he had left out.

"Yes, he has two sons by his mistress," Rupert admitted, flushing despite himself.

He had once had a French mistress who said the most shocking things to him in bed and yet she had never made him even the slightest bit embarrassed. In this moment, however, his cheeks heated.

"That must be difficult for his wife. Does she know?" Lizzie asked politely, her tone not one of condemnation or disregard, but of calmness.

Rupert's face darkened again. Yes, she knew. He had heard their rather nasty conversation a couple of months ago. His sister-in-law had been begging her husband to return to her bed and his brother had stated that he was sick of bedding a woman who couldn't conceive a son or give him any pleasure in the bedchamber. Then the countess had started screaming about her husband's whore and Rupert had left the house.

He nodded tightly, unable to talk about the private conversation he had accidentally overheard.

"Well, I sincerely hope my next husband doesn't keep a mistress. I'm not sure I could handle the betrayal."

Rupert quickly got on the defensive, thinking of what his brother must have endured, going to an unwilling wife's bed. He had never bedded a woman who didn't want him, and he wasn't sure he could if he had to do so. Another reason why marrying a *suitable lady* for him was a most disturbing idea.

"Well, it really depends on the man. Most men consider mistresses to be vital for their sanity," Rupert announced, in as casual a manner as he could.

"What is that supposed to mean?" Lizzie asked, looking horrified.

"I mean that a lot of wives hate going to bed with their husbands. Would you blame your husband for seeking out another woman in that case?" Rupert asked, leaning back against the park bench, one arm outstretched. He couldn't believe he was having this conversation with Lizzie.

"I would never deny my husband," Lizzie burst out, blushing furiously when Rupert gave her a rather meaningful look.

"Yes, dear lady, but would you *enjoy* it? There's a big difference between duty and enjoyment." He smiled knowingly. His point had been made.

Lizzie looked as though she were ready to jump to her feet in outrage. Just as he thought she would do so, she stilled instead and looked at him in thoughtful silence for a moment.

"That is something my next husband can discover for himself," she declared, sticking her nose in the air in the ultimate gesture of obstinacy.

Rupert burst out laughing, stopped, looked at her face and then exploded with laughter again.

"You make me laugh so much. However do you do that?" Rupert wiped a tear away from his eye. He hadn't laughed properly in such a long time. It felt wonderful. His belly fluttered with happiness and an unaccustomed lightness filtered through his body.

"Well, I am glad I provide you with something to laugh at." Her tone was dry, but a tiny smile hovered about her lips. "Perhaps you would walk me to my carriage, Rupert?" Lizzie tentatively used his name for the first time. Warmth spread through him at her use of his Christian name. Were they friends now?

She waited for him to offer his hand and help her to stand up.

Rupert jumped to his feet, and took her hand with what he hoped was courtly grace. They walked slowly back to where their carriages were waiting, companionable silence between them.

"It was lovely talking to you, ma'am," Rupert said, bowing and chastely kissing her knuckles before he handed her up to her carriage door.

"It's Lizzie," she said quietly, smiling at him with true kindness. She really was an amazing sight to behold.

"Lizzie," he repeated, and as he watched the retreating vehicle, his heart thumped fast. Even faster than the beat of the horses' feet as they carried his new friend away.

Chapter 5

"The Spares" still met on a regular basis. Despite Oliver now being the Duke of Lincoln and Archie being the Earl of Tother—his honorary title until he inherited the Marquessate from his father—Rupert still thought of their group as "The Spares," the name they had acquired when it had consisted solely of younger sons of aristocrats.

They met at their club for drinks often and tonight was one of those occasions.

"How is my sister?" John asked Archie, throwing a card down in front of him. They were playing poker, not for money but simply for fun. Rupert was competitive by nature, but the other three weren't and they never wagered any money.

"She is well, John." Archie quirked a brow at his childhood friend who was now his brother-in-law. "She misses you. Why don't you join us for dinner tomorrow?"

John shifted in his chair and dropped his gaze to his cards again.

"I'm not sure of my arrangements tomorrow but thank you for the invitation," John replied, giving no indication of whether he would accept or not.

Rupert shared a confused look with Oliver, both of them feeling the cutting knife of unease settle in the silence.

"Sarah misses Charlotte even when they don't meet for a day. It's amazing how close they have become." The Duke of Lincoln spoke thoughtfully of his wife.

Archie's brown eyes softened again as they did every time his wife was mentioned.

"I know. I am very happy that they get along so well. This means our sons will grow up together, just as we did." Archie smiled fondly, looking at John again who still refused to look up from his cards.

"Another drink?" Rupert asked gruffly, oddly moved by what Archie had said. He had never thought about it like that. Oliver and Archie had sons only a year apart. They would grow up together. Go on holidays together. Begin school together. As the youngest son, he had never been able to play with anyone. He had been extremely lonely.

"Definitely," John replied, lifting his hand to call a footman, who brought over the whiskey decanter.

"More?" Rupert asked the other two, who were still nursing their second drinks. John and he were at least into their fourth, with many more to come, Rupert was sure.

"No, no," Oliver and Archie both chimed in, moving their glasses out of Rupert's reach.

"Why, you old fuddy-duddies," Rupert scolded good-naturedly, pouring himself a drink.

"Can't have another in case the wife finds out?"

Archie smiled his secret smile and Oliver sighed.

"Unlike you gentlemen, I wish to be sober enough to please my wife in bed tonight." Oliver joked, his smile showing how much he was looking forward to the task.

Rupert laughed but John choked on his whiskey. Gone were the days that they joked about their mistresses; now they were joking about their wives. How times had changed.

"But hasn't Sarah given birth recently?" John got the words out before coughing roughly to dispel the whiskey that had found its way into his lungs.

"It's been two months," Oliver reminded him, smiling whilst he sipped his own whiskey.

John stared at Rupert in obvious horror. Rupert stared back and shrugged. He had no idea how long you had to wait before the bedding process could continue. He had always assumed one had to wait at least a year, but then again, what did he know about love matches? Or the birthing process and its aftermath. Perhaps it wasn't necessary to wait that long. Looking at the shared glance between Oliver and Archie, Rupert guessed he had been mistaken about having to wait a year.

John poured himself another huge whiskey and downed half of it. Rupert blinked. What was wrong with John tonight? He was obviously bent on forgetting the world. Rupert recognised the signs well.

"Are you serious?" John asked again, obviously unable to believe what he was hearing.

Oliver laughed at the look on John's face and even Archie smiled again.

"The doctor said six weeks." Oliver shrugged casually but couldn't wipe the smile off his face.

John took another long drink and looked at Archie. "You t…t…t…oo?" he asked, slurring the question.

"Do I need to be sober enough to please my pregnant wife, or did I only wait six weeks, too?" Archie asked, in a rare show of sly humour.

John turned beet red but resolutely held Archie's stare. "The six weeks bit."

Archie shared another glance with Oliver. "Six weeks was more than long enough," he drawled, in another rare show of his masculine side.

Archie had been a virgin for so long, he had never joined in on any of their conversations when they had discussed women in the past. Rupert had always secretly wondered if Archie enjoyed it as much as they did once he finally started. Now it seemed that he did.

John gurgled in his throat before saying, "I am truly shocked."

Rupert burst out laughing with Archie and Oliver. John did look shocked. His eyes were glassy and his hair was unkempt. When had that happened?

"Just wait until you are married too, John. You'll know all these things firsthand."

"Hardly. *If* I ever marry, my wife won't be the only woman I will bed."

Rupert chuckled at John's arrogance. He had also thought similarly. He wasn't so sure he wanted that anymore. Looking at Oliver and Archie, they both appeared to be the happiest of men.

There wasn't a gentleman at the club who looked happier or healthier than those two.

Archie and Oliver both frowned at John's words but said nothing.

"I think it's time to go home," Oliver announced, drinking the last of his whiskey. "My entertainment will be wanting to go to sleep soon."

Rupert grinned at his friend. That was one way of talking about the blonde-haired angel whom Oliver had married.

Archie rose too. "I also need to be getting home."

Rupert sighed. Gone were the days that the three of them would be trying to drag Archie by the scruff of the neck into a brothel. They'd never achieved it and now that he had Charlotte, they never would.

"Looks like it's just you and me," John said to Rupert, dragging his coat on.

Rupert watched John stagger around with some envy. Rupert was considerably bigger than all of his friends, so he needed a much larger amount of alcohol to become intoxicated.

John led the way out of their club and they hired a carriage to take them to a local up-market brothel. The building had heavy curtains drawn across every window facing the street. Light shone out dimly from the glass, the brightest being the window to the right of the front door. Rupert knew that one was the sitting room where most of the girls sat, waiting to be chosen.

Rupert was as randy as he had ever been, but he stopped at the front step. How was he going to do this? He had spent the past week thinking about nothing other than Lizzie. Was he really going to assuage that lust in another woman's body?

John called out, "Come on!" from the front door and Rupert walked up after him.

The madam greeted them with familiarity, giving them a generous smile and a warm greeting. They were good customers.

John quickly picked a young brunette with large breasts and staggered out of the sitting room with her.

Rupert sat on the chair he was offered and looked about the room. It was the first time he had looked at anything other than the girls. The room needed a good cleaning and some work done on the plaster. There was also a nasty smell coming from one side of the room where someone must have vomited recently.

Rupert crinkled his nose in displeasure. He suddenly felt like leaving.

"Who would you like, Mr. Willoughby?" the madam asked, sitting on the armrest of his seat and stroking his arm. She saw his hesitation and changed her approach.

"I have a new girl I have been offering only to special customers."

She clicked her fingers and a young girl appeared. She would have been just older than sixteen and had hair the colour of Lizzie's. She smiled shyly at him and dropped her shawl so that he could get a better look at her half-clad form. She was in little more than a chemise. Her skin was beautiful and her breasts pert and well-shaped. Rupert perused her happily and waited for his body's reaction.

Nothing.

He chuckled to himself. He was in a room with more than ten women, all with their charms displayed for his pleasure and he felt absolutely nothing. His cock didn't stir. He sighed.

He wanted Lizzie. His body twitched at the mere thought of her and he laughed, out loud this time. If he pictured Lizzie, he could take this new girl. He could do that. He wasn't letting himself be emasculated by a woman he barely knew.

"I'll take her," Rupert announced, throwing back the last of the cheap whiskey the madam had poured for him.

The young girl's eyes widened when she saw how big Rupert was, but she resolutely turned and led him out of the room.

Rupert stumbled behind her down the hallway, glad she didn't have a room upstairs. He wasn't sure he could manage stairs in his current state.

The young prostitute moved into a dimly-lit room that was clean by a brothel's standards. Rupert took a moment to enjoy the silence, then he began to undress. Jacket, cravat and shirt were dumped on the floor.

The young girl's eyes widened again, but this time Rupert saw less fear and more excitement her gaze. He knew his body was pleasing to most women. They often told him he was strong and muscular.

She lifted her skirts and lay back on the bed, displaying a beautiful pair of young, smooth thighs and pubic hair the same colour as that on her head.

She smiled gamely and held out her arms to him.

Rupert stifled the need to roll his eyes. He wasn't ready, nowhere near ready.

"I need you naked," Rupert told her gruffly, clearing his throat loudly.

The girl blushed pink. *Heavens, she really is new!*

She stood up and began unlacing her chemise. She had very little on except the chemise and a bulky skirt. Both were pooled around her ankles within moments, her need to please both reassuring and disconcerting.

She shivered visibly and Rupert's heart sank, as did any level of arousal he had acquired. He couldn't do this. She was barely old enough to be here, but she did have a gorgeous young body. Pert little breasts topped off by red nipples, a flat stomach and long legs. She was lovely. But he couldn't get his body to respond.

Get a grip, you pansy. Rupert dropped his pants, displaying his flaccid penis.

"Lie on your stomach," he told her, moving over to the bed so he could stand behind her.

The girl did as he asked and spread her legs a little for him. Rupert closed his eyes and pictured Lizzie. His blonde-haired, brown-eyed girl. Her face swam into view and Rupert imagined her smile, her lips parting as though she wanted a kiss from him. His body stirred to life.

Rupert opened his eyes and ran his hands over the beautiful derriere of the girl in front of him, enjoying the satin-smooth skin and soft flesh beneath his fingertips. She turned her face slightly so that he could see her profile and the momentary stirring dissipated instantly.

His senses came alive as though he had been sobered with a bucket of cold water. He could smell the other men who had been in this room. The girl in front of him wasn't Lizzie, and she didn't want him for anything more than the money she would be paid. He was absolutely disgusted with the whole situation—but most of all, with himself—to the very depths of his stomach.

He hauled up his pants and grabbed his jacket and shirt.

"Thank you," he yelled and, still half-undressed, he broke out the door. He couldn't stay in that room a moment longer. He'd truly embarrass himself if he did.

The madam walked into the foyer to see who was making such a racket, her eyebrows high in surprise when she saw him. Rupert tucked his flaccid penis back into his breeches and hastily dressed.

"Mr. Willoughby, if she isn't what you want—" The madam began, with an angry glint in her eye.

"She was lovely, beautiful. It wasn't her at all. I just can't tonight..." Rupert did not the poor girl to be punished for his lack of focus. He threw too much money at the woman, flung open the heavy door and rushed out into the clean air.

Dishevelled, embarrassed, but relieved to be out of there, Rupert took a big breath and shook his head. With a heavy sigh, he gestured to a passing hackney carriage and made his way home.

Chapter 6

Lizzie had been almost yawning through a casual evening of socializing, until she heard a woman over her shoulder sigh and say in a gushing tone, "Oh, he came. I hoped he would."

Lizzie somehow knew who the woman was talking about. She could sense Rupert's presence as he entered the room.

She closed her eyes, fighting the urge to drop her head into her hands. She knew Rupert was a rake. Every woman in London seemed to know him intimately, but did that fact really have to be thrown around like the latest fashion? Lizzie had assumed that such knowledge about a gentleman would make him distasteful. Unfortunately, nothing about Rupert seemed to be off-putting. Instead, the knowledge of how desirable everyone found him made her nervous and the fact that he seemed to still be pursuing her despite all her refusals to play his game, made her excited. To admit anything less would be a lie.

She enjoyed the interest in his eyes and the feminine satisfaction of having such a masterful male want *her*.

Lizzie turned to the elderly lady beside whom she'd been sitting and asked her a question about how she had enjoyed her dinner. It took every ounce of effort she possessed to focus on the woman, but for the life of her, Lizzie didn't hear the words.

Lizzie refused to look as he walked over to her, but her skin goose-bumped in uncomfortable awareness nonetheless. It was infuriating that a man could have such an effect on her. Infuriating, and intriguing.

"Mrs. Symmons," drawled the amused voice from behind her.

She quelled the instant smile that sprang to her lips and instead rose to her feet and turned. There he stood, all six feet, four inches of male, muscle, and strength. She tilted her head to look up at him and offered a tiny smile.

"Good evening, Mr. Willoughby," she greeted, aware of others watching and making sure she curtseyed appropriately.

"Would you care for a turn around the grounds, Mrs. Symmons? The gardens are very fine in the evening air."

"Thank you, sir, but I would much prefer to visit the music room. Do you know where it is?" she asked.

It was quite obvious to her that Rupert never had to pursue a woman before. He had none of the normal subtleties. He was playing a very straightforward game. Like a bull at a gate, he had her in his sights and he was charging.

Lizzie had known that the first thing Rupert would try to do when he saw her again, would be to lure her somewhere private. Although Lizzie had a feeling that she would enjoy being alone with Rupert, perhaps staying inside the house with others around them would be safer for her sanity and her reputation.

"I do, indeed, Mrs. Symmons," Rupert said, offering Lizzie his arm and drawing her close as they walked in search of the music room. His size and warmth made her knees shake a little, the need to lean on his strength deep within her.

"Are you enjoying yourself tonight, Lizzie?" he asked, as they walked along the hall and entered the music room.

Her heart thumped when she realized the room was vacant.

"I *am* enjoying myself, thank you, Rupert," Lizzie answered, allowing her hand to fall from his arm and walking to a wall where several string instruments were mounted. She needed distance to think more clearly. Her need for a husband and indeed, a well-built man, was beginning to make itself far too clear to her.

"Do you play, Lizzie?" Rupert asked, running his hand lovingly over the keys of the pianoforte.

Her laugh rang clear in the air, too loud as always. She closed her mouth and put her hand on her belly to stifle the trembling deep within her.

"I wish I did. My mother didn't believe it worth the time to practice music, but languages? Yes, she would abide me practising those."

She smiled at the memory of her many language lessons. Her late mother had been an unusual woman and Lizzie still missed her so much, it hurt.

Rupert's brows rose. "How many languages do you speak?"

"Not many," she lied, then laughed again as though he had told a good joke. She was certain he really didn't want to know. Most men found her intelligence intimidating and some insulted her, calling her a bluestocking.

Rupert growled, coming up to grab her and tickle her in the

ribs as though she were a child. Lizzie twisted away, giggling despite herself. She had rarely been tickled, even as a child. What a strange thing for him to do.

"You told me you cannot abide lying. Now, tell me how many languages you speak," he demanded, scowling with what looked like mock outrage. Lizzie took a few steps back and found the wall pressed into her back. Rupert had stalked her right to edge of the room, but despite her earlier reservations about his dishonourable intentions, she didn't feel at all scared.

Instead, his closeness called to her; pulled her in.

They were alone now, but what would happen if someone walked in? She put her hands up to rest upon his chest, making no move to push him away. His chest was warm and rock-solid, and her imagination ran wild. What did he look like, beneath these clothes? Her thoughts created heat in her cheeks. But still she did not withdraw from touching him.

He leaned closer, bringing his hands up to her face and tipping her so their lips met. Her eyes widened as his mouth brushed against hers, softly, almost reverently.

Lizzie held herself very still as the warmth of his full lips caressed hers. A wonderful stirring of pleasure rose in her belly. Determined to get full measure from this kiss, which must surely be a once-off, she rose up onto her toes and threw her arms around his neck as she had seen her maid do once to one of the footmen. She pressed her mouth more firmly against his and clung, hoping he would know what to do next. She had rarely been kissed by her husband and didn't quite know what else to do beyond this moment.

He dropped his hands to her hips and pulled her into him. She could feel his hard flesh and that instantly caused a spark of arousal to course through her. Rupert dipped his tongue into her mouth and she moaned at the pleasure. The sound seemed to encourage him. He plundered further; deeper.

Lizzie was swept into the most amazing kiss of her life. Rupert was holding her as though he desired her desperately and kissing her as though she were the only one he'd ever wanted. She kissed him back as enthusiastically as she knew how, wanting to share the pleasure with which he had filled her. Stroking his tongue with her own, she gripped his black, shoulder-length hair in her hands, threading her fingers through it.

"The music room is this way, I believe." A female voice came from outside the room and down the hallway.

Rupert and Lizzie both heard it at the same time. Quickly breaking apart, Rupert rushed across to a bookcase, presenting his back to the doorway to make it look as though he were searching for a book.

Lizzie took a moment to realise she needed an occupation and saw a pack of cards on a small table. She quickly hurried over to pick them up and began shuffling as she dropped into one of the chairs surrounding the table. She was breathing faster than normal and hoped her flushed cheeks and rapid heartbeat wouldn't give her away.

A gentleman and two ladies walked into the room without knocking. They were all elegantly dressed. The younger lady, a pretty blonde, seemed to know that she was attractive. There was a confidence in her manner that spoke of self-assurance.

"Rupert," she cooed when she saw him, then sauntered over to the bookcase and wrapped a proprietary hand around his elbow.

* * *

Rupert's stomach plummeted. Of all the rotten luck! Well, at least thanks to Elise's presence, his erection, the one to beat all other hard cocks, was instant history. He should remember that trick if ever he needed it again.

"Elise," he sighed, trying subtly to disengage her hand from his elbow.

She finally removed it with a pout, but grazed her nails over his arm whilst she did. Rupert suppressed a shudder.

"Elise, we'll meet you in the parlour?" The older, darker-haired lady enquired, moving toward the door with a sly smile.

Elise nodded and smiled her thanks, then turned stony eyes on Lizzie.

Despite her obvious unease, Lizzie started laying out the cards on the table in front of her to start a game of Patience.

Rupert saw the look in Elise's eye and knew he was in trouble. He had barely spent a week in her bed before moving on. She was vain and selfish, and he had been turned off her soon after their first night together.

"Rupert, I have missed you. Would you escort me home tonight?" she purred softly. Not so softly that Lizzie wouldn't hear, but enough for it to appear that she was attempting to be discreet.

Rupert didn't dare look directly at Lizzie, but he could see her out of the corner of his eye. She hadn't stopped in the dealing of her cards, but he knew she had heard Elise's offer from the obvious stiffening of her spine.

For one second, he considered taking Elise up on the offer. It was true that she was a rather nasty woman, but she would let him sate his desire in her body all night if he wanted. He would finally be rid of some of this tension. It had been weeks since he'd lain with any woman and Lizzie was driving him half out of his mind.

Lizzie, the woman who wanted marriage—a breed of woman that Rupert had sworn not to pursue. Why was he even bothering with her? Rupert knew that if he left with Elise, then he would never get the opportunity to be intimate with Lizzie. That's all it would take to ruin his chances with her completely.

Looking down into Elise's eager face he realised he wasn't ready to give up on Lizzie. He may not want marriage, but this overly-willing woman would not fill the need inside him. It went so much deeper than the needs of his body. He didn't know how to articulate what he wanted, but somehow, he knew that Lizzie held the key.

"Thank you, Elise, but I'm afraid I already have plans for this evening," he lied smoothly.

Elise's eyes flickered a warning. She glanced at Lizzie again.

"I can wait. Shall we meet later in the week, then?" she asked, her mouth setting into an angry line.

At that moment Rupert realised he would never bed Elise again, and that it be best for everyone if he let her know it.

"I'm afraid I'm no longer available, Elise," he answered, giving her a direct look that would have had most men running from the room.

"You cannot be serious, Rupert!" Elise replied plaintively, looking back over at where Lizzie sat, playing Patience. She placed both hands on her hips and her face began turning red.

"Tell me that little mouse is not the reason for denying me," she demanded, pointing at Lizzie.

Rupert clenched his jaw and inhaled sharply through his nose.

"Mrs. Symmons has nothing to do with the situation, Elise. Leave her out of this. I am not interested in you anymore. Find someone else to escort you home," he added, before walking over to Lizzie and sitting in a chair opposite her.

"May I join you at cards, ma'am?" he asked calmly, pleased that he had managed to rein in his temper.

Lizzie merely nodded and gathered up the cards on the table before handing him the pack.

Rupert eyed her and knew he was in trouble. Elise had been easy to deal with, although he knew she hadn't given up on him. She was like a dog with a bone, that one.

Lizzie was a completely different type of lady. She seemed deep in thought, no longer lost in feeling or as carefree and happy as she had been before Elise walked in. He was in deep, deep trouble.

"I'm sorry you had to witness that," Rupert apologised. He had always relished his rakehell reputation, as it gave him free rein to do what he wanted, whenever he wanted. No one ever expected anything from him, except a good time while it lasted. For the first time in his life, he actually wished his reputation wasn't quite so obvious. How was he going to gain the trust of this beautiful and sincere person when women were practically seducing him in front of her?

"I'm sure it happens often enough." Lizzie shrugged as if uncaring, but her sad face drove home the truth. She wasn't unmoved by what had just happened.

Rupert smiled politely, not quite sure how to handle this situation. Frequently, he'd had jealous ladies competing for his attention and even several ex-mistresses in one room at once. It had been rather entertaining. This was very different. For the first time ever, he actually cared about what the lady in front of him was thinking and feeling.

He wanted to make her happy, not sad.

"Shall we play poker? I assume you know how to play," he said. As an army widow, he assumed she'd likely know a number of card games.

Lizzie stilled. "Of course, I know how to play poker."

Rupert grinned at the acerbic edge in her tone, and dealt the cards, relief coursing through him in calming waves. Were they back on an even keel once again? He hoped so.

"Do you have a current mistress, Rupert?"

His head lifted in shock, staring at the lady who had just asked one of the most forthright questions any woman had ever asked him. He swallowed awkwardly, not knowing how to answer honestly and still retain Lizzie's company.

She sighed, the sound tugging at his heartstrings in a painful way. "And I suppose you gamble and drink often as well?" She continued with her questioning as though he had already answered the first.

He opened his mouth, but nothing came out. Should he just ignore the mistress question and answer the second one? He swallowed the lump in his throat once again and smiled gamely at her.

"Not as much as in my salad days," he admitted. There was no gentleman who didn't gamble and drink. It was the excesses that would be a problem.

"Thank you for being so honest," Lizzie said, with a slight tremble in her tone. She stood up, dropping her hand to the table.

Panic fluttered in his chest, like a caged bird.

"Lizzie, please don't leave," he urged, reaching out to grab her by the wrist. She couldn't leave now, surely? Did she find his past so abhorrent?

"It has been lovely getting to know you," she said politely, pulling out of his grasp before doing something extremely odd. She leaned over and cupped his cheek, in a brief caress of tenderness.

Rupert leaned into her touch without thinking, his eyes

closing of their own volition as warmth spread through his heart. When her hand dropped away, he jumped to his feet in a panic. This couldn't be over. It just couldn't.

"I haven't visited my mistress since I met you. I swear it," Rupert told her, uncaring that he was now begging.

Lizzie smiled sadly, shaking her head as she backed away toward the door.

"But for how long can you wait? I may never be ready and you'll go and visit her and I'll be devastated."

A vise-like clamping around his heart caused Rupert to press his hand to his chest. She cared; she really did. He had succeeded in affecting her as deeply as he himself was affected by her, but now he didn't know what to do. He had hurt her.

"I don't want any other woman, Lizzie. No one but you arouses me anymore."

Lizzie simply raised a questioning eyebrow, and then walked to the door.

Rupert stood transfixed, a victim of his own machinations.

"You didn't answer the question," he forced out of his almost-frozen lips, before she disappeared.

Lizzie turned and frowned at him.

"The languages. How many?" he prompted, and her frown cleared.

A glint appeared in her eyes as she smiled softly.

"Five," she answered.

Impossible.

"English, French, Gaelic, Italian and Latin."

He gaped at her. What woman spoke so many languages? She really was a rare gem indeed. He strove for a nonchalant smile, though his heart was aching at the thought she would soon be gone.

"Latin?" he said, raising his eyebrows.

"My parents were scholars," she whispered, before leaving the room. She pulled the door shut behind her with a gut-wrenching finality.

Rupert fell back into his chair with a loud sigh, staring up at the ornate ceiling as if it could provide much-needed assistance.

Yes, he had a mistress, a woman whom he had visited often, initially. However, those visits had recently dropped back to almost fortnightly. Rupert had been thinking of giving her up when Lizzie had dropped into his life and now, he wished he had paid the woman off weeks ago.

He did gamble and drink occasionally, but that didn't mean he was like Lizzie's husband. He would never ignore Lizzie so that he could go out enjoying himself.

He was getting ahead of himself again. What was it about this woman that had him almost ready to jump down the church aisle? Maybe it was her unrelenting determination to accept nothing less than marriage. Either way, Lizzie was different. But could he marry her? He hadn't planned on marrying for several years more and then he had planned on a traditional marriage of convenience, not the love match his friends had found.

Love match?

Where had that thought come from? He desperately needed another drink.

Chapter 7

Rupert requested his butler obtain Lizzie's address, before he went to bed and fell asleep with a heavy heart. He wasn't sure what he was going to do if he found her, but he couldn't sit idly by and allow her to walk out of his life forever.

The next morning, he was woken at a most unlikely hour, his head pounding from lack of sleep.

"I'm sorry to disturb you, sir." Rupert's butler apologised, laying a letter next to his head.

Rupert groaned and stretched, disoriented. What time was it? It could barely be dawn.

"What is it?" He grumbled, rubbing his hands down his face and groaning again as he blinked slowly awake.

"I have news about Mrs. Symmons and thought you may want to know as soon as possible."

Rupert shot up straight in bed and snatched for the letter on his pillow. Sleep forgotten, his body began to hum with happiness. Had the butler found her already?

"Tell me now," Rupert demanded, ripping open the letter in impatience.

"Mrs. Symmons received a missive yesterday requesting her presence at a country estate in Kent. Her estate, I believe."

His heart sank at the news.

"She's gone." His shoulders dropped and the letter fell to the sheets. How had his butler found out this news in such a short space of time?

"I believe it is only for a few days, sir." The butler nodded impassively, but remained standing beside him as if he hadn't finished imparting his information.

Lizzie owned a country estate? Why did he not know this? Perhaps herlate husband had left it to her. Or her parents.

"Is there anything else, Grimmit?" Rupert asked impatiently, glaring up at the starched man.

"The estate is several hours' drive away, sir. If you wanted to surprise the lady, perhaps, you could arrive for lunch?"

Rupert's nervous belly did a little lurch and a skip. He nodded and smiled up at the man standing above him.

"Order a bath, if you would, Grimmit."

The older man's lips kicked up in a rare smile and he bowed out of the room.

Rupert leapt out of bed and pulled on some drawers. Stretching out his back, he began pacing restlessly within his room. The servants brought in his bathtub, then left to retrieve hot water.

He walked over to the window and opened the curtains, letting daylight into his usually dark bedroom.

He couldn't leave things as they were between him and Lizzie. He needed to tell her why he was the way he was, and perhaps explain why it would be advantageous for both of them to indulge in a brief affair for their mutual pleasure. She had responded well to his kiss and he knew he could give her so much more pleasure in the bedchamber if she allowed him the time.

"Today is the day," he vowed, watching the sun rise over the far hills for the first time since he was a child.

Upstairs in her bedroom, Lizzie was having her hair arranged by her ladies' maid when the housekeeper burst in, all-a-flutter.

"Ma'am, you have a visitor!" The elderly woman before her practically bounced as she spoke, unable to contain her obvious excitement. The overly plump lady was flapping her hands like a bird.

"A visitor?" Lizzie repeated, handing her maid a pin from the dresser and trying to hide her smile as she envisioned her housekeeper as a goose at Christmas luncheon.

Who would be visiting me? She had only arrived late the day before. Surely gossip in this part of the country couldn't be quite so speedy?

"Yes. The Honourable Mr. Rupert Willoughby has called on you."

Lizzie's heart flip-flopped and she gasped as panic

descended. He couldn't really be here, surely? She swallowed the lump in her throat and turned away from the mirror.

"Did you say... The Honourable Mr. Rupert Willoughby?" Lizzie repeated slowly.

The housekeeper nodded, her face flushed like a teenage girl's.

"Tall, well built, wavy hair..." Lizzie began.

"And bright black eyes," the housekeeper finished for her. "Pardon me, ma'am."

Lizzie sighed, and let the hand that held another pin, drop into her lap. It had to be him. No one would know of their association enough to say it as a joke and no one else looked like Rupert in any way. He was certainly striking, especially with those eyes.

Lizzie stood up on legs that were suddenly a little shaky. She'd had a great deal of time to think on her carriage ride to the estate and during the previous night, when she'd barely gotten any sleep. Something strange was happening to her. All she could think about was that kiss and how it had made her feel.

She wanted Rupert. She finally admitted that to herself as the sun rose this morning. She desired him on a physical level that she had never experienced before. She had never believed she could feel such things.

Perhaps it wouldn't be *such* a bad thing if she had a short affair with this gentleman before she remarried. She had no one else in mind as yet, as no one had caught her attention in any way.

Maybe he could teach her about passion and about the pleasure that was to be found in the bedchamber, if such a thing was to be pleasurable at all. Lizzie was sure that Rupert would know. It may also help her in keeping her future husband happy and secure. Perhaps it wouldn't, but Lizzie knew she didn't want to miss out on this very rare opportunity.

Rupert had made it crystal clear he was not the marrying type and she wasn't sure that she would even want a man like him as her husband. He was wild and irresponsible. He probably couldn't support himself, let alone a wife. There was evidence to the contrary, of course, but she didn't want to think too much on the virtues of the Honourable Rupert Willoughby. She already liked him a little too much. If she happened to fall in love with a rake, then she would indeed turn out to be the fool.

She looked once in the mirror to check her hair and dress, to see that her appearance was respectable. There was nothing opulent about her attire, but she looked neat and tidy. She smoothed the material at her waist and descended the stairs.

"The gentleman is waiting to see you in the sitting room, ma'am," the butler told her with genuine warmth. His old, wrinkled face lit up with a rare smile.

Lizzie suppressed the need to groan. Why was everyone so happy to see her getting attention from a male? It wasn't like he was a suitor.

"Thank you, Leaves. Mr. Willoughby is a friend from London who has travelled up with some news, I believe. Would you be so good as to show him to the dining room and make sure there is an extra place for him at luncheon?" She barely succeeded in keeping a straight face as she told the white lie. This butler had known her since she was in the nursery and it was a little embarrassing to have to explain to him who Rupert was, despite the innocence of their association thus far.

"Of course, my lady." The man bowed, looking a little disappointed at her explanation.

She tried not to sigh and headed into the dining room. The

cook had prepared for an army as usual, and for once, Lizzie was excessively grateful.

She sat at the head of the table and folded her hands in her lap, her breath shuddering as she struggled to maintain her calm. He was here and they were essentially alone.

The door opened and her suitor strolled in, his morning clothes pristine despite the travel.

"Mrs. Symmons, please forgive my intrusion." Rupert bowed to her, then walked around to her end of the table.

Lizzie let the smile spread across her lips, unable to keep the happiness that his mere presence elicited inside her. It was amazing how different she felt here, in her home. It was almost as though London had been stifling her desire for this man. Here, where she was warm and safe and happy, her feelings were blossoming like a rose in spring. And he had only been in her presence a few seconds at most.

"Not at all, Mr. Willoughby, you are very welcome. Please join me." Lizzie gestured to the chair opposite hers.

"It looks as though your cook anticipated more than one person for lunch," Rupert commented, glancing down the table as though he expected more guests to arrive.

Lizzie laughed as Rupert's eyes swung back to her.

"Not at all, my lord. My cook enjoys her employment, and I am here so infrequently nowadays that she spoils me when I am."

"Ah," Rupert sighed, obviously relaxing as his shoulders dropped and a soft smile replaced the stilted grimace that had been there before.

"How was your journey?" Lizzie enquired, helping herself to warm chicken and roast potatoes. She had long ago told her staff she could serve her own food at the table, at least when she dined alone. Or almost alone, in today's case.

"Oh, it was very pleasant, thank you," Rupert answered conversationally.

They chatted about the different methods of travel over lunch, happily eating and relaxing in each other's company. It was the worst possible thing for Lizzie's desire to have a simple affair with this man, as she could see herself doing such a thing every single day.

"Would you care to go for a ride, Rupert? I have a horse in my stables that you may like." She had to stop herself from imagining him as a husband. He was an acquaintance who found her desirable. Nothing more than that.

Rupert's eyebrows shot up rather charmingly. Lizzie chuckled at his surprised expression and waved him toward the door so that she could go upstairs and change.

"Please see the butler for whatever you need, and I will meet you at the stables in ten minutes."

Rupert fought the urge to swing Lizzie up into his arms and charge up the stairs with her. Did she understand the innuendo behind what she had said? Was she offering a ride of the sort he would like? Or did she seriously own a horse that could handle his weight?

It seemed the latter was the truth.

The rather stern-looking butler directed him to where he could borrow some riding pants and a shirt. Both articles of clothing were an uneven fit, but Rupert couldn't bring himself to care about his appearance. He would usually be dressed beautifully to ride. He had the latest style of riding clothes in his residences, styles that sculpted his large frame perfectly. None of that mattered with the adrenaline pumping through his system today. He was so excited to see what Lizzie had in store for him. She had been noticeably warmer at lunch and he could barely suppress the manic grin that wanted to spread across his face as he headed out to the stables.

They were very well maintained, with several staff on hand. Lizzie lived very comfortably indeed.

"I see you found our stables, Rupert." Lizzie greeted him with a smile as she walked into the building that housed her horses.

Rupert's breath caught in his throat and all he could do was nod at her. Her riding jacket was slightly too tight and curved around her ample breasts like a lover's caress. She looked so delicious he wanted to drop to his knees and eat her up right there in the hay. She was so tiny he could have picked her up and carried her home, but again, there was a strength in her that he was determined not to ignore.

"What horse do you have that you think can handle me, Lizzie?" Rupert asked lightly, trying his best not to put too much innuendo into his question. She was, after all, a true lady and he had no desire to offend her if she didn't mean anything by her offer.

"This one," Lizzie announced in a similar light tone, opening the door to a stable further down the row.

Rupert stepped forward. Inside the stall was a huge bay stallion. He was restless and pacing, in obvious need of exercise.

"He's beautiful." Rupert marched close, unable to keep the awe from his voice as he reached out a hand and stroked the stallion's neck.

Lizzie smiled and entered the stall with him.

"You couldn't have surprised me at a better time. This fellow is on loan for breeding purposes, but he almost injured one of the mares yesterday. The grooms have been saying that he needs a good, solid ride to settle him down and yet none of them are game."

Lizzie smiled up at him and again Rupert wondered at her words. Did she know what she was inviting when she talked of such things? He could give her a ride that would ruin her for every other man she would ever meet in future.

"Luckily I decided to call on you, then," Rupert agreed, treading carefully.

"Yes, it is." Lizzie walked over to a stall opposite and signalled to one of the grooms.

"Please saddle up Thunder for Mr. Willoughby and have Rose readied for me." She pulled on her gloves with practiced ease.

Rupert smiled at her use of the horses' names.

"Rose?" he enquired, envisioning a sweet little mare for his sweet little lady.

A moment later the two horses were presented to them and Rupert gaped up at them. The mare Lizzie was to ride was almost as big as the stallion they had for Rupert.

"Lizzie, you can't possibly ride a horse that large," Rupert exclaimed, looking down on her dainty head and wondering how on earth she was going to handle such a creature.

Lizzie thanked the groom and allowed him to hoist her up into the saddle. She swung her leg over so that she could ride astride like a man, and gave him a smile that could only be called flirty.

"I can handle a large animal, sir," she said. And with that, she turned the huge mare around and broke into a trot.

Rupert laughed out loud at her feisty word play and swung up onto the massive stallion. He hadn't ridden in the country for months and was looking forward to a punishing gallop. London had so many rules, he had barely been allowed to canter in town.

He trotted up next to Lizzie and called out, "If this stallion is in a rut, is it safe to have your mare so close to him?"

Lizzie laughed again, her lovely long hair blowing in the breeze behind her. Rupert shifted in his saddle as his body throbbed and his skin heated. There was no other woman he would rather be with. Her laugh was the most magical sound in the world and gave his very soul pleasure to be around.

"Rose is his mother. She won't put up with any nonsense."

As though to prove Lizzie's point, Rose snapped her teeth at her offspring and he slowed down to match her gait.

Rupert laughed out loud, surprised to be having such a good time. In fact, he couldn't remember the last time he had felt this happy.

"Ready?" Lizzie asked, turning Rose's head so that they faced an open and empty field.

Rupert turned Thunder in the same direction, nodding in agreement, despite not knowing exactly what she had in mind. He was ready for anything.

Lizzie squeezed with her thighs and dug in her heels. Rose surged forward with a grunt and broke into a gallop.

Rupert gripped the reins and his heart picked up the animal's bruising pace. If she wanted this horse ridden hard, then so be it.

He flicked the reins, dug in his heels and the powerful body between his legs surged forward.

Lizzie leaned over Rose urging her to go faster.

Rupert's body stirred at the sight of Lizzie's thighs spread and her bottom in the air. He kicked his stallion harder. The powerful body surged and raced ahead. Rupert let the horse have its way. He ran through a thicket of trees and clear across another field. Sweat trickled down his brow and he wiped it away, eventually pulling the horse back to a trot. The horse, too, was breathing hard, but seemed fit and ready for more. Rupert turned the horse and noticed Lizzie standing, leaning against a tree watching him from half a field away.

He flicked the reins onto the horse's flank and charged over. He loved the feel of a horse's body. The warmth, the power and the thrill of the speed. *What an animal!*

He crossed the same field again and made his way back to where Lizzie stood. He circled around her a couple of times until she laughed and twirled to keep up with him. That was when he jumped down. Unable to resist, he picked her up, kissed her hard on the lips and set her down again.

Lizzie's eyes widened and then she smiled hesitantly.

"It seems you enjoyed that," she said.

"I did, thank you. It has been a long time since I got to ride such a magnificent animal." Rupert ran his hand over the horse's neck and lovingly patted its rump.

The stallion flicked his head once, as though in approval and walked off to join his mother in a feed of grass.

"Is this your husband's estate?" Rupert asked, not wanting to be rude but curious all the same. Had she married money?

"No, it is my father's estate."

Her answer had no bearing whatsoever on their relationship, although it could make her prey to a fortune hunter if it became known in London that she was a widow with means of her own.

That thought made him frown and he shook it off. He didn't want to think about what would happen tomorrow to his widow who was searching for a husband.

"You seem happier here than in a ballroom in London," he remarked, taking in her flushed cheeks and the easy way she stood. She looked healthy and happy and unfortunately for him, even more beautiful than he had ever seen her before.

Lizzie laughed, her eyes shining at him as the melodic music of her laughter surrounded him.

"I love it here. If I had a choice, I would rarely visit London."

"Really?" Rupert asked, surprised. Most ladies he knew would never leave London if they didn't have to do so. They would always spend the first weeks of the season complaining about how bored they had been in the off-season, and how much shopping they needed to do.

"Do you really love London so much?" Lizzie asked, averting her eyes.

"Oh, no, not me." Rupert said. He enjoyed the diversions of town, but he was always relieved to return to his family's country estate post-season. Six months in London was quite enough.

"I haven't met many ladies who prefer the country to town."

Lizzie looked up, cocking her head to one side.

"Well, sir, perhaps you have not been associating with the right sorts of ladies."

She shied away and Rupert berated himself for accidentally bringing forward the topic of his experiences with other ladies.

He walked over to where she had trounced off, and pulled up her chin so that she had to look at him.

"Perhaps I haven't," he agreed, using his other hand to pull her into him.

Lizzie's hands came up to his chest and she tiptoed up to meet his lips. Rupert captured her sweet mouth, sighing in bliss. It was so good to have his hands on her again. It was not just good; it felt *right*.

A rumble of thunder sounded in the distance and Lizzie pulled away from Rupert's embrace.

"We'd better get back before it starts pouring." She sighed and walked over to the horses, rearranging her clothing on the way.

"Race you back to the house," she said, laughing as she ran over to Rose.

Rupert followed and effortlessly hoisted her up onto her saddle. Striding back to his own horse, he quickly mounted. He could smell the rain now; it wasn't far away.

"Let's go!" He flicked his head at the house and grinned like the devil himself. She'd better ride fast. He couldn't wait much longer to get his hands on her.

They rode back at a punishing pace, the drop in temperature and slight sweetness to the air forcing them to move quickly. The heavens opened up just as they arrived back at the stables.

There was only one groom on duty and he took both horses inside to care for them.

"We'll wait in the adjoining stable for the rain to stop if you need us," Lizzie called out to the groom, ducking out into the rain to run across to another outbuilding.

"Make sure you don't need us," Rupert said in a forceful tone, making it clear to the young groom that they wanted to be alone. The man nodding in understanding as he led the horses back for a much-needed rest.

Rupert stalked after Lizzie through the heavy rain, stepping into the clean, spare stables and shaking his hair. Lizzie had removed her wet coat, hat and gloves and was inspecting her riding habit for damage.

Rupert ripped off his own jacket and stepped purposefully toward the woman who had been tormenting him with desire for weeks.

Chapter 8

"No, I want to talk," Lizzie cried, bringing her hands up to the large chest in front of her and pushing him back. If he started to kiss her, she would never be able to say what she needed to say.

Rupert's full mouth compressed into a thin line, but he nodded and stepped back.

Lizzie sat down upon one of the hay bales and gestured for Rupert to sit also. He was far too tall for to remain standing if she was seated. Lizzie felt like a pixie next to him. He was as big as an oak, and just as dense if he thought she would allow him to treat her the way he had treated his other ladies.

"Tell me how you found out where I was and why you left

London to come here and see me," Lizzie demanded, looking directly into his brilliant blue-black eyes. She was learning to read his face and didn't want to miss any subtle changes in expression.

Rupert blinked.

"I didn't like how we ended our conversation the other day and I hoped to change your mind."

"But you still don't wish to marry," Lizzie reiterated, making sure that they understood exactly where the other stood on this topic. Her needs hadn't changed in that department, though she may be ready to rethink her strategy.

"No," Rupert whispered, almost regretfully.

"Tell me why," she said quietly, knowing that Rupert pretended to be a classic, thoughtless, unfeeling rake, but she could sense that he really wasn't so. She was convinced that she couldn't desire someone with no heart, no soul, and no feelings for others. There had to be more to him than what seemed obvious to others.

"Marriage is for men who want to stop living the life they have," Rupert spouted, throwing in a charming smile. That was an attempt to escape her interrogation, she was sure.

"Do you still see your mistress?" Lizzie asked, watching his face carefully, ready to pounce on any sign of lying.

"No," Rupert told her, looking her directly in the eyes.

"Why not?"

She knew that Rupert had convinced himself that he wasn't ready to marry, but if he had given up his mistress just so he could be with her, didn't that indicate a stronger than normal desire?

"We had tired of each other." Rupert smiled charmingly and Lizzie saw the truth in that statement. However, he wasn't telling her the whole truth. She could see his eyes were shadowed. There was something he didn't want her knowing, she was sure.

"Do you have a new mistress?" Lizzie asked, as lightly as possible. Could he have found someone else in the past few days?

"No, not yet," Rupert said quietly, his eyes beginning to burn.

"Why not?" Lizzie asked, pushing for more information. It seemed that he was willing to change his life for her, travelling out of London and giving up his mistress, but for how long would this last?

"Because I want *you!*" Rupert declared, with soul-burning intensity.

"Only me?" Lizzie asked, standing up on shaking legs.

Rupert twitched uncomfortably, obviously not liking where the conversation was heading.

"Lizzie…"

"Only me?" she repeated, this time more demand than question.

Rupert nodded sharply and Lizzie mimicked the move, happy in part.

"Tell me why you don't wish to marry," she asked again. If she was going to throw away her morals and indulge in a purely physical affair with Rupert, then she needed to know more about him.

"I told you–" he began, his eyes flashing.

"No, you lied to me. Tell me the real reason," Lizzie demanded, all five feet, four inches of her body rigid and determined to ascertain the truth.

* * *

Rupert looked away and tapped his fingers against his knees for a moment, then finally spoke.

"Because, unless I can have a marriage like Archie's and Oliver's, I don't wish to marry."

"You think it's impossible to have a union like those of your friends?" Lizzie asked, surprised he felt that way. Surely Rupert could see that if his friends could find happiness, he could do so also.

"Not impossible, but a love match is rare in our society. The norm is to be trapped into a marriage as are most of the *ton* gentlemen, or even into a forced marriage owing to circumstance. I don't want a union... like my brother's." Rupert all but whispered the last words.

Lizzie let a breath out slowly, her heart aching at the pain she heard in Rupert's words, but she pushed forward regardless. She needed to know why he was so terrified of the one thing she craved so much.

"Tell me, why is the thought of a love match and subsequent marriage so horrible?"

His lips twisted and his brow furrowed. "My brother's marriage started out with mutual affection, but as the desire for a male heir brought more and more daughters, any real feelings that were once there between them turned to hatred," Rupert explained, almost choking on the words.

"Is that why you are so adamant you don't want to marry yet? You don't want to be your brother's heir, so you're letting it turn you off marriage entirely?" Lizzie's mouth fell open.

That was not rational, although she understood his abhorrence to the weight placed upon him. Since his brother had failed to provide a legitimate male heir, Rupert would now be responsible for siring the next Earl of Sweeting. He would hate to have that forced upon him, especially if it meant marrying for a reason other than love, as his friends had.

"But your brother has five daughters. Can't daughters also inherit their father's estate in the absence of a male heir?" asked Lizzie. "Why shouldn't the next incumbent of the Sweeting estate be a countess instead of an earl?"

Rupert shook his head. "Tradition," he replied. "The title of our house has always been carried by a male heir. Anything else is unthinkable."

"This bias against female heirs is ridiculous," said Lizzie, with passion. "Traditions have to change."

"They won't change so easily," replied Rupert. "Not in our time, at least. Can you imagine how ridiculous it would be to have the title holder of the Sweeting estate unable to attend to her duties because she is confined due to pregnancy?"

"I would love it if you could have the courage to say that to our friend Charlotte, the Countess of Tother," said Lizzie drily. "She hasn't allowed pregnancy to confine her one little bit. She'll be the next de facto Marquess of Hunting, mark my words. Besides, have you forgotten? England has already had several queens. Queen Elizabeth was one of the greatest sovereigns England has ever produced. So how can your brother allow this bias against females to destroy his marriage and pressure you? I think it's ridiculous." She sniffed to show her disgust.

"Ah, Lizzie, good Queen Bess was a rare exception. She was uncommon. The truth is, a male heir is always better for the family, the estate and the entire country. Female heirs in general just de-stabilise the natural order."

Lizzie's anger rose at Rupert's words, but she decided to keep it in check for the present time at least.

"Marriage is so final. Even if you don't suit with someone,

you're stuck with them for life," Rupert muttered, standing up and staring out the window, brushing dirt from his palms.

"That is very true." Lizzie sighed. She knew that only too well. Even in the few months she'd been married, she had often wished she hadn't been tied indefinitely to a man who would rather bet on a horse race than spend an evening with her.

Rupert turned to face her suddenly, his eyes blazing with passion. He wet his lips with his tongue. She could feel her gaze drawn to the fullness of his bottom lip.

"We'd have something so much better, Lizzie. We could spend time together, talk, and enjoy each other's company. And then part if we tire of each other." He urged her to consider what he said, opening his hands with his palms up in a gesture of hope.

"And if we didn't tire of each other?" she asked, voicing her most worrying concern. Lizzie knew Rupert would most likely get tired of her once he had enjoyed her body a few times, but she wasn't so sure she would feel the same way. The man in front of her was changing, and his beauty was now shining brighter than it ever had. He was as honest as a child, as passionate as a rogue. He was a man she could love with all her heart and if he couldn't love her in return, she would surely be crushed.

Her question still hung in the air.

"Then, we marry." Rupert choked out these words, his discomfort evident as he shuffled his feet.

"That simple, is it?" Lizzie asked, placing her hands on her hips as anger continued to stir in her belly. What if she, after spending time with him, decided she didn't want to marry him? Had he thought about that? Big rake that he was, could she trust him not to break her heart every night he didn't come home?

"Would you not marry me if asked?" Rupert cocked his head to the side as he stepped closer to her.

"I don't know, and you won't either unless you ask in earnest," Lizzie shot back, annoyed that he couldn't see how much more she wanted from him. She may have been content with lukewarm affection from other gentlemen, but from Rupert, she would require his whole heart.

"I am the heir to an earl," Rupert explained, with a smooth voice and a smile, oozing *tonnish* charm and creeping closer still.

Lizzie wanted to laugh at his attempts to charm her, but stuck her nose in the air instead.

"I don't care about any of that. I have money and an estate. I want a man who loves me, Rupert. Who desires me..."

"I desire you!" Rupert growled, now within touching distance.

"My body you desire, not me as a person," Lizzie reminded him, annoyed despite her resolution not to be. She was so much more than a lump of flesh to be fondled, didn't he see that?

"No! I desire a woman who can speak five languages, is honest as the day is long and wants children beside her, not just in the nursery!" Rupert growled again, unknowingly spouting off the words that would draw her in completely. Did he understand her? Could he want her for who she really was?

Lizzie swallowed the uncomfortable lump in her throat. She couldn't take it anymore. He was so close now; she could feel the heat of his breath and her body ached with need for him.

"Kiss me, please." She couldn't take any more of this banter. There was no one around to hear them or see them and she wanted nothing more than to feel his arms around her.

Rupert moved forward and swooped, his lips diving to capture hers. He wrapped his strong hands around her waist and lifted her high. She instinctively wrapped her legs around his middle and opened her mouth to his searching tongue.

Finally, something inside her cried, and they each moaned in unison.

Rupert kissed her deeply as he walked the few feet to one of the stable walls and pressed her up against it. The wall was dirty and hard, but Lizzie didn't care. She needed him closer. He held her there with one hand under her bottom and using his other hand, tugged down her bodice to give him access to one breast.

Lizzie cried out as he exposed her nipple, arching her back to encourage his touches. He dipped his head and licked the tip, suckling her gently.

"Oh, Lizzie, I want you so," Rupert groaned against her skin, thrusting his pelvis into Lizzie's open thighs and pressing her higher on the wall.

Lizzie moaned in response and tugged on Rupert's hair so that he would bring his lips back to hers. She needed him everywhere. Her mouth wanted his kisses, her breast wanted his touches and between her legs, she was beginning to feel wet and hot and very uncomfortable.

Rupert thrust his tongue into her open mouth, and she sucked on the hard muscle, drawing it deeper into her. She broke away, panting as she ground against him.

"Yes, Rupert, please." Lizzie panted, unable to breathe. She was on fire. Rupert's hardness was pressing against the sensitive spot between her legs. She had never realised that area could be so sensitive, but he was giving her pleasure already. Liquid fire raced in her belly. She needed him there. She had never felt like this before. Lizzie finally understood why people coupled for more than procreation.

Rupert continued kissing her, pulling away only to dip his head and draw her breast back into his mouth. Lizzie arched her spine to give him unrivalled access and rotated her hips to entice him further.

Rupert groaned, but did not move to touch between her legs, where she was aching for him. Lizzie began to thrash. She was ready to bed. What else could she do to encourage him to hurry up? She needed him, and he didn't seem to feel the same way. Why wasn't he laying her down to join with her?

"Please, Rupert," she begged again, pulling his face back up to her so that he could look into her eyes. Frantic brown met smouldering blue. Then something strange came over Rupert's face, something desperate.

"Tell me you want me," he demanded, rucking up her skirts in hard, measured tugs until he was pressing against the slit in her thin drawers.

Lizzie moaned and tilted her pelvis in an invitation as old as time.

Rupert gasped as his fingers came into contact with her skin, his gaze snapping up to meet with hers.

"Where do you want me?" he asked almost incoherently. Lizzie understood him.

"Here," she panted, pressing one of her hands between her legs and in return caressing him. She ran her hand over him and marvelled at the hardness there, feeling an intense kick of female satisfaction when Rupert closed his eyes and moaned in obvious pleasure.

"What do you need, Lizzie? Tell me," Rupert urged again. Lizzie heard the words, but could barely understand him. She knew the tone, though.

"This, please," Lizzie panted again, caressing him boldly over his breeches once more. This time, she concentrated on the hard, rather considerable length of flesh beneath her palm. She flattened her hand against him and realised she didn't cover most of him. Was she going to be able to do this?

An inhuman noise rumbled out of Rupert's chest, and Lizzie

practically heard his control snap. Holding her effortlessly against the wall with his body, her legs wrapped tightly around his hips, Rupert tore open his breeches. Lizzie cried out as the coiled tightness in her belly built up.

His fingers probed the slit in her drawers and then he ripped open the material, cold air drifting over her hot, wet nether regions.

Lizzie could feel the violence in him, in the tremble of his shoulders, the rock-hard strength of his body. Instead of being afraid of his strength, of what he could do to her, she revelled in it. She encouraged him to an even greater need. She wanted him to want her as much as she wanted him, to the exclusion of all others. She moaned when his warm and gigantic hands cupped her bare buttocks and positioned her. Apprehension made her still. She wanted him desperately, but would it be as uncomfortable with Rupert as it had been with her husband?

No, this would be different. She was sure of it!

The worry flew out of her head as quickly as it had arrived when Rupert ran his fingers between her legs, rubbing her over and over again. She jumped and gasped as heated sparks tingled in her legs, in her belly, making her nipples ache and her insides throb with wanting. Lizzie couldn't help the moans that bubbled out of her throat, a pleasure that was unknown to her until now, coursing through her veins, her body clenching in anticipation of what was to come.

Rupert gripped her hips and positioned her body so that the head of his engorged penis lay at her entrance. He pressed in slowly. Lizzie grabbed tight to his shoulders as he slid in effortlessly, her tight, wet core gripping him. The ache inside her body sighed in relief, but there was more to come, she was sure of that. Rupert grunted and plunged to the hilt, burying himself completely within her tiny body.

Lizzie gasped in surprise and clung tighter to the man in her arms. He was so much larger than her husband had been. The breadth and length of him was almost overwhelming. Her greedy body welcomed him. There was no pain, only pressure and an incredible feeling of fullness where she had been empty and aching.

Rupert stilled, thankfully, holding himself there, deep inside her body. The feeling of fullness relaxed and the need in her belly still tugged at her.

Rupert seemed to be shaking from the strain and gasping for breath.

"Are you feeling all right?" he asked, gruffly.

Lizzie saw the concern and something odd fluttered near her heart. He cared. Despite the fact that he was buried deep inside her, he had stopped to ask about how she was feeling. He hadn't continued what he'd been doing. He was waiting for her to say it was all right. She had expected pleasure from a man as experienced as Rupert, but she had not expected so much care. Tears of surprise and joy came to her eyes and silently slipped down her cheeks.

Lizzie watched Rupert's face crumple. He shifted as though he was trying to dislodge her. That wonderful feeling of fulfilment and fullness was about to be taken away from her. She cried out in distress, and her body clamped down on him. Internally, she was pulling him back inside and externally, she was wrapping her arms and legs around him like a limpet on a rock.

"No," she cried, grabbing his jaw with both hands and pulling his face back to hers. She kissed his surprised mouth and pulled back only a tiny bit so that she could whisper against his lips, "I need you, please don't stop."

Rupert stared into her eyes as though determining her

honesty, his gaze wide and searching. Then his mouth tightened, and he grabbed her arse, thrusting back into her, hard.

Lizzie didn't dare look away. His blue gaze watched her with such intensity she was afraid he'd stop if she dared to close her eyes.

A moan fell from her lips. He thrust in again harder. He was moving slowly, controlling each thrust, angling her hips to rouse her body.

Lizzie was dying, she had to be. Nothing had ever felt so right. She could feel the pleasure in every part of her body. Her hands burned, her toes were curling and that place between her thighs he was pleasuring, was alight.

Lizzie started screaming. It was too intense. She wouldn't survive this. She tilted her pelvis to meet his, to try to take him in deeper.

Rupert groaned against her, pounding harder.

The tension within her belly wound as tight as a spring. Rupert was pushing her higher and higher up an unknown hill. Then he thrust once more, and she fell. Off that hidden cliff edge, into an abyss that caused her body to spasm and convulse, and the greatest pleasure she had ever known washed over her.

Rupert gripped her hard and bellowed in pleasure as he pulled out of her body and shook in her arms. He turned so that his back was against the stall door and slid to the floor.

They landed with a light thump and Lizzie couldn't help the giggle that escaped her. Rupert normally looked Herculean-strong, yet at this precise moment, he looked as happy and vulnerable as a child.

Chapter 9

Rupert forced his eyes to open and took in Lizzie's happy, flushed, and shining face.

Unable to resist, he kissed her long and deep, feeling himself stir beneath her bottom. Lizzie pulled back and her expression changed. Her previously ecstatic eyes widened and a new smile replaced the old.

Could he want her again? So soon after being sated? Impossible! She wiggled her bottom, and his flesh twitched and began to stiffen. A deep groan escaped his throat as blood began to pulse through him yet again.

Lizzie unwound her beautiful legs from around his waist and

placed her knees on either side of his thighs. The heat of her skin and the intense look in her eyes made him grab her hips tightly. She rocked her pelvis back and forth, her still moist body caressing him in slow, agonising strokes.

Her moan was soft, ending in a gasp that hit him right in the gut. He was rising to meet her and when Lizzie angled herself so that he was rubbing over her lips, Rupert threw his head back against the wall. Lizzie closed her eyes and began to raise herself up, until his cock was cold and needy, then slowly she impaled herself on him.

It was agony. A beautiful, sweet, torturous agony. The longer he watched her face twisting in bliss, the more he couldn't believe what was happening. He had only just experienced the most mind-numbing sex of his life and now, only moments later, it was happening again.

Lizzie's eyes flew open as she moved up and down on him, riding him as one would a horse. He'd never experienced anything like it. She threw her arms around his shoulders and pulled his head toward hers for a kiss.

The kiss ignited between them like port thrown on a fire. Tongues mating, parrying and thrusting as their bodies moved in unison. Rupert couldn't sit there without moving one second longer. He gripped her hips and started moving her on him. Up and down, faster and faster, bucking beneath her in a matching rhythm. Her breath hitched and soft moans of pleasure erupted from her throat. Keeping the rhythm going with one hand, he reached between them with the other and pulled up her skirts. Crisp curls and slick flesh met his searching fingers, and he rubbed the area above their joining. Lizzie cried out and arched her back, pushing herself down onto his hand as she rode him harder and harder.

The amazing rush to orgasm began to tingle in the back of

his thighs, the heat rushing up his back. Determined not to finish without her, Rupert flicked his thumb over her, faster, even as he pumped his hips to make her move along with him. It was an awkward rhythm to maintain, but he refused to leave her wanting.

Lizzie's gasps got louder and louder until she stopped with a strangled groan and her channel began convulsing all around him, begging him to join her. He moved faster and let the orgasm steal over him, his head exploding in a shower of light as heat poured through him.

Damn! Quick!

He pulled out from the slick heat of her body, his seed pulsing between them, over her skin and turning his legs to jelly.

Even as his orgasm was still rippling through his body, he marvelled at the fact he had barely removed himself from her body before it had been too late. He had always controlled his orgasms.

When he had begun, he'd asked one of the women at the whorehouse about preventing bastards. She had laughed at him but had taught him to pull out before he released his seed. He was usually excellent at getting a full measure of pleasure whilst still having control over where he spilled himself. He had never pulled out so late before.

Thanks to the position they'd chosen, she'd surely be covered in his essence. Cringing, he wrapped his arms around her and planted a kiss on top of her head where she'd collapsed against his chest.

She didn't stir.

"Lizzie?" he whispered, but he was only answered by her soft, even breathing.

Rupert let his head fall back against the stall door and held her tighter in his arms. It was so good to hold her like this. He had never spent the night with a woman before, even with his permanent mistress. He always preferred to go home to sleep in his own bed. The intimacy of sleeping together was always a step further than what he wanted to share with any of his women.

With Lizzie, though, he had the sinking feeling that if they were anywhere near his home, he would carry her to his bed, curl around her and fall fast asleep.

The thought had him moving. Old habits die hard and his fear never really died.

Rupert lifted Lizzie gently off him and lay her down on the straw. He stood up on shaky legs and fastened his breeches with fumbling fingers. Some of the fastenings were ripped, so he pulled his waistcoat down to cover the damage.

Lizzie's beautiful, sleeping face made his chest ache. Could he really have a good marriage like his friends had? Is this how it had begun for them, too? Strange feelings of tenderness with a person you had just met? Of everything being right with the world, despite it all being new?

He righted Lizzie's bodice again, regretfully tucking her perfect breast away. Lifting Lizzie up into his arms, he was amazed again at how light she was. She stirred briefly whil he carried her toward the house and lifted questioning eyes to his.

"Ssh, I'm going to tell them you have a headache and need to lie down. Just close your eyes," Rupert crooned to her, grateful in a somewhat cowardly way that he didn't have to deal with the aftermath at this moment.

She nodded gently, tucked her head into his neck and fell into a deep sleep.

* * *

The next day, Lizzie relived every moment of her time with Rupert in the stables. She even found herself running her hand between her legs during her bath, just to see why and how she had felt those moments of pleasure. She found she could, in fact, elicit some feelings using her own fingers, but it was nothing as intense as when Rupert had touched her.

The difference between the moments with Rupert and the bedding she had experienced with her late husband was immense. Her husband would lie between her legs, thrust into her despite her discomfort and leave soon after. It wasn't degrading or embarrassing as her friends had described it. He had found pleasure in her body and that had been enough.

Now, she knew what her husband must have felt at the end when he would flood her with his seed. That was also different. Rupert had pulled out of her body at the end and spilled himself on her skirts rather than inside of her. She assumed it was to prevent conception, although after being married for a year without any pregnancies, Lizzie feared that she was barren. Either way, his actions were thoughtful and showed his caring nature.

He was gone by the time she had awoken from her nap and in some ways, she'd been glad. She wanted time alone to sort out her feelings and she had to complete the few matters that had called her to her country estate in the first place.

She would be back in London for a ball the following night and she couldn't wait until she saw him again.

* * *

Rupert sat in his study the following afternoon, drinking his port very slowly. He had been over and over each moment of his encounter with Lizzie in his head and he still couldn't work out why it had been so different with her, so soul-shattering.

He had slept with every type of woman imaginable. Some were sensual and active in their attentions. Other women preferred a more passive role. Some of the more experienced women had even pleasured him with their mouths and whispered erotic words into his ears.

Nothing in his past had ever caused an orgasm that compared to the two he had experienced the previous day. He had barely touched her, and had been completely dressed, yet the urgency, the pleasure and the passion had been unsurpassed by any other encounter.

Why? He wanted to know. Was it the lack of bedding in the previous month? And if that was so, why was the second orgasm with Lizzie, moments after the first, just as good? Was it her? It had to be. She was beautiful and had a perfectly shaped body, but it was something more than that. Something in her aroused a passion in him, a response from him that had never been called on before.

Rupert couldn't wait for their next encounter. He would be in control this time. It would be in Lizzie's bed where he could kiss and touch her until she screamed. He smiled to himself, seeing in his mind's eye the tears of joy Lizzie had cried at their initial joining. Which is what they were, he had realised later. At the time, he'd been so horrified that he might have hurt her. Rupert could still feel the ache where his heart had cracked a little.

He sighed and rubbed that part of his chest where he still felt it. Something about this whole tryst was different. He wasn't sure if he was going to come out on the other side as the same man. He'd never been so obsessed with a woman. Even during those times when he had regular mistresses. He would dally with married women who offered themselves to him, but he had never been possessive. With Lizzie in his life, he desired no one else. And the idea of her being with another? He couldn't even entertain the thought!

Tomorrow he would meet her again and his fate, it seemed, was in the hands of the gods.

* * *

"What are you doing here, Rupert?" John asked, as he walked into the Somerville ball. Dressed in his best evening clothes, he could barely contain the excitement simmering in his blood. Lizzie would be here. He was going to see her again.

Wiping his face of any signs of emotion, Rupert raised an eyebrow at John.

"Why wouldn't I be here? There are ladies aplenty."

John huffed next to him.

"Come, get a drink with me. I think Oliver and Archie are in the card room."

Rupert looked around the crowded room and found Lizzie in a heartbeat, his gaze going toward her like a homing pigeon.

"I'm sorry, no. If you'll excuse me, John." Rupert didn't wait for an answer from his friend, but headed straight into the thick of the crowd. His heart was pounding in his chest as he stepped up to the small group of ladies surrounding Lizzie.

"Mrs. Symmons, may I have the pleasure of this dance?" Rupert bowed to where Lizzie stood, along with Charlotte, Countess of Tother and Sarah, Duchess of Lincoln, the wives of Archie and Oliver.

Lizzie gave him a coy smile and held out her hand.

"Of course, sir," she answered, not even bothering to look at

Sarah and Charlotte. Rupert, on the other hand, could see their amazed expressions.

He swung Lizzie into his arms and started waltzing her around the room. It felt so good to have her in his arms, he had to quell the urge to whisk her straight off to a place where he could have her all to himself.

"Are you wearing your drawers?" Rupert asked Lizzie, mostly to shock her. He certainly succeeded. Her eyes grew round and an involuntary gasp left her open mouth. Then she smiled.

"Are you?" she asked, with a flirty flutter of her eyelashes.

Rupert burst out laughing and several gentlemen turned around to look.

Sobering quickly, embarrassed by the attention, Rupert danced her away from anyone close to them.

"You didn't answer my question, ma'am," Rupert scolded.

"Neither did you answer mine, sir," Lizzie reminded him with a grin.

Rupert's cheeks flushed with heat.

"Of course, I am," he answered.

"Well, so am I," Lizzie returned, giving him an enchanting smile.

"Could you leave them at home next time?" Rupert asked, pushing his luck with her good mood.

"Would you like that?" Lizzie asked, frowning.

"Yes, I would like to know that you are naked beneath your dress, waiting for me and no one else knowing about it," Rupert confided, smiling as though he was joking. Inside, though, he was shocked at himself for asking. She wouldn't do such a thing for him. Would she?

"Is that a common request of yours to your mistress?" Lizzie asked, as if striving for sophisticated nonchalance. "I've never requested it, no," Rupert answered slowly. Why would she ask such a thing?

"What's wrong?" she asked, eyebrows drawing together.

"You aren't my mistress," he declared, feeling like he should tell her the difference if she didn't already know. The word mistress for a woman such as Lizzie didn't suit. It would be degrading.

"Then, what am I?" Lizzie asked, cocking her head

"You're my lover," Rupert corrected her.

"What's the difference?"

"Money, mainly," Rupert admitted, ruefully. Most of his other mistresses had lived in a house he permanently rented in a cheap part of town. Otherwise, they were married or widowed and still received gifts of jewellery and the like.

"I don't want your money, my lord."

"What do you want then, Lizzie?" Rupert asked, his mood serious for once.

"You," she answered quietly.

His heart did a dance in his chest and his throat constricted. He'd never heard any words so sweet. Did she want only him? That had to be a first in his life. No expectations, no needs or requirements?

Rupert finished the waltz with a courtly bow to his beautiful partner and began walking her back to her friends.

"May I escort you home tonight?" he asked politely, pitching his voice not to be heard by other guests nearby.

"No," Lizzie answered with a smile.

Rupert's smile faltered and he opened his mouth to utter a sentence that would indeed sound like a whine.

"You can meet me there later," she explained, giving his hand a squeeze and slipping a calling card into his palm. She curtseyed and made her way back to the other ladies.

Rupert watched her go and discreetly slipped the card into his jacket pocket. He made his way to the card room and barely felt his feet touching the floor. He had gotten everything he had ever wanted. At that moment, he couldn't have been happier.

Chapter 10

Lizzie fiddled and bounced in her seat the whole carriage ride. She was glad she had asked Rupert to meet her at home as she couldn't possibly have allowed people see them leave together. But she knew that he would have kept her entertained on the carriage ride.

She hurried up the steps to her front door and it opened even before she knocked.

"Ma'am," her butler greeted, taking her pelisse, hat, and gloves.

He stepped closer and lowered his voice.

"There is a Mr. Willoughby in the study, ma'am. Would you

like me to show him to the sitting room?" The old butler seemed unsure about what to do. Lizzie faltered for a moment. This was the same man her father had hired to look after his home years before. Her throat tightened and her cheeks warmed. She was embarrassed to admit she had a man visiting her. Well, that had to change and her butler would have to get used to the idea. As did Lizzie herself.

"No. My chamber. In about fifteen minutes please, Saunders." Lizzie spoke breathlessly.

To his credit, the old butler's expression remained reserved.

"Of course, ma'am."

Fifteen minutes later, Lizzie was dressed in her sheerest nightgown with her hair unpinned and falling down her back.

Rupert knocked but didn't wait for a response. Instead, he quickly entered the room. He seemed as restless as a caged animal.

He stopped in his tracks when he saw her seated at her dressing table, his eyes widening, then he began undressing.

First his jacket, waistcoat, and cravat, then he pulled off his boots and stockings. He left on his shirt and breeches and started toward her.

Her belly tightened, and her hands trembled as she moved them restlessly in her lap.

He was here. Finally.

"Are you feeling... well?" Rupert asked, his brow furrowing.

Well? Lizzie smiled and stood up, closing the short distance that separated them with a few quick steps. Her arrogant big man wanted reassurance that they were making the right decision. She could see it in his eyes.

"I am very well. I am looking forward to this, Rupert," she whispered, reaching out for him. She finished unlacing his shirt and pushed the material from his shoulders. It was like unwrapping the best gift she had ever received. She'd never been more excited, not even on her wedding day. Her heart raced and a squeal caught in her throat.

Tonight was going to be spectacular and there was no downside, no risk. She knew Rupert would take care of her.

As the shirt fell away, Lizzie gasped, taking a few moments to catch her breath. Rupert had a body that rivalled the ones she had once seen in a pugilist match. Huge shoulders and massive, muscular arms. Did he box to maintain his physique?

Lizzie could stand still no longer, running her hands up his arms and over his chest in absolute enthrallment. He had a light covering of almost black hair over his golden skin and she had the sudden urge to kiss every inch of his chest. Still too shy to do so, Lizzie contented herself with exploring the warm skin beneath her fingertips and smiled coyly up at the man who was allowing her to caress him in such a brazen style.

Rupert held perfectly still and Lizzie stepped so close there was no gap between their bodies. She rose up onto her tiptoes and pressed her lips to the hollow between his collarbones, savouring how warm and soft his skin was. Lizzie flicked her tongue out very gently to taste the skin there and was rewarded with a groan from Rupert as his hands came around and roughly grasped her bottom. Only two layers of silk kept his hands from her skin.

"Ssh," she whispered, stroking his chest with her hands. "I won't hurt you." She didn't know where the words came from, but she felt like she had captured a wild beast, unused to the touch of a human. She didn't believe he was afraid of the physical side of things, but she sensed that he was skittish about any tenderness she might want to show him.

Rupert closed his eyes and shuddered under her caress.

She moved her hands to his breeches, unfastening them

quickly and pushing them down his hips in one swift move. She had to slide down his front to accomplish this and found herself eye to eye with his impressive manhood. She was amazed that his huge organ had fit inside her so well, but fit it had. Twice already. She looked up to his face, but Rupert's eyes were still closed.

Unable to resist, she pressed a single, soft kiss to the large head of his organ, thanking it for all the pleasure it had given her two days before. Rupert's breath hissed between his teeth and Lizzie loved the fact that she was affecting him so much.

She stood up again and ran her hands over his chest, amazed that he was allowing her to take such liberties with his body. Her husband hadn't even removed his nightshirt when he had come to share her bed. Now she had this amazingly virile, naked male in her bedroom and willing to let her explore with him.

Lizzie stepped around Rupert's massive frame, running her hands lightly over his back and down to his sculpted behind. He was truly magnificent; like a warm, live sculpture of marble come to life.

Rupert raised his hands and pushed her nightgown off her shoulders. She let it slide all the way down to her feet and stood in front of him, unashamedly naked. There was no need to be silly or embarrassed. She had, after all, been married and there was no need to feign modesty now.

A feral growl rolled out of him as he picked her up and placed her gently in the centre of the bed.

Lizzie lay back against the pillows, not lifting her hands to cover herself. She had never been completely naked in front of a man before and certainly not with the candles still lit. Rupert had shared himself with many beautiful women. Would he desire her still? Or would she come up short in the comparison?

Rupert shook his head.

"Am I all right?" Lizzie asked nervously. Perhaps she was too small? Or her breasts not full enough?

"All *right*?" Rupert croaked. "You are the most beautiful woman I have ever seen." He dropped a kiss on her lips and she frowned. Lying wasn't necessary. She was already in bed with him. He didn't have to seduce her now.

"You don't have to lie, Rupert. I'm not going to turn back now," Lizzie assured him, a little disappointed.

Rupert laughed. A true, deep chuckle.

"Lie? About what? Look at my face, Lizzie."

Lizzie dragged her eyes up to meet Rupert's, his lie still hurting her inside.

"You are the most beautiful woman I have ever seen," he repeated with emphasis, speaking slowly and clearly.

She stared into his brilliant blue eyes and watched for any tightening of his mouth or ghosts in his eyes that would indicate an untruth. All she saw was fire.

"Kiss me," Lizzie whispered, sliding her fingers into his shoulder length hair and gripping the back of his skull.

Rupert slid on top of her and captured her mouth in a profound and possessive kiss.

Her head spun. As if he sensed her overwhelm, he moved back, then down her body, urging her legs apart. He took one of her nipples into his mouth and she arched up, wanting him closer. Rupert sucked and gently bit one of her nipples. When Lizzie moaned, he lifted his head and gave her a devastating smile.

Lizzie smiled back and turned her body so that he could do the same to her other breast. He laughed and bent his head to her eager flesh again. He made his way down her body, gently kissing and licking every inch of skin that he found along the way. When Rupert hit upon the centre of her, he planted a kiss on top of the dark blonde hair there.

"Rupert, are you sure you should be doing that?" Lizzie asked, faintly mortified that his face would be so close to that part of her. She tried to close her legs, but he wouldn't allow it. She began to cover herself with her hands, but he held them to the side. Lizzie felt panic rise. This could not be correct behaviour.

Rupert laughed at her modesty and ran his tongue around the bit of flesh just beneath the parting of her lips. Lizzie screamed in acute pleasure, grabbing handfuls of the quilt on either side of her, but no longer trying to stop him.

She couldn't believe how amazing what he was doing to her felt. His tongue was playing havoc with her flesh and she was tightening on the inside as she had done during their time in the barn. She started panting, feeling herself pushed toward that amazing plateau of pleasure.

Rupert stilled and pulled himself up so that he was face to face with her.

"Not this time," he murmured, licking her lips and giving her a taste of what he had loved.

"I want us to come together," he announced, moving his hips into position.

"Come?" Lizzie repeated not quite understanding what he meant. She had been so close to that ultimate pleasure; why had he stopped?

Rupert clenched his fists on either side of Lizzie's head and plunged into her. He buried his head into her hair and groaned.

Lizzie yelped in surprise at the deep and sudden penetration. She became accustomed to him very quickly and wrapped her legs around his hips and slid her hands around his back.

Rupert began moving, slowly at first and she moaned in time

with his thrusts. She had never experienced such feelings before. How could this man turn her into such a wanton creature, who revelled in every move and thrust of his body?

"Rupert, I'm going to..." she groaned into his ear, her back arching so that her pebbled nipples brushed his chest. She didn't know what was happening to her, but she was about to fall into that sea of rippling flesh and pleasure.

Rupert thrust harder.

"Come for me, Lizzie, now," he groaned.

Her body quivered and shook and then she cried out, convulsing around him. He pulled out of her once again and hot seed spurted onto her belly as he groaned loudly, warmth sliding between them.

Lizzie gripped his sweaty back, holding him down, keeping him with her, terrified he would leave.

Rupert collapsed onto his side, breathing heavily. He reached across to the wash stand, pulled close to the bed. He wrung out a wet cloth and carefully cleaned Lizzie's soft belly. She watched him from beneath half-closed eyes and waited for him to finish.

Sleep pulled Lizzie under its dark cloak, and she wrestled to stay awake a moment longer. She curled onto her side in her sleeping position and bumped her bottom against Rupert's side. He stilled for a few moments, neither moving away from her nor getting any closer.

Then the heat emanating from his huge body wrapped around her and dreams from Heaven came down to greet her.

Chapter 11

Still half asleep, Rupert was warm and comfortable, dreaming about a minx wriggling on his lap. As the last of the darkness wore off, and he blinked his eyes fully awake, he realised the minx in his lap was real. The soft weight of her breast filled his palm, her delicious bottom pressed against his morning erection.

How was he still in Lizzie's bed? He never stayed the night. His valet would wonder where he was. Shaking his head to dislodge that strange thought, he kissed Lizzie's shoulder in greeting and started to roll away from her.

Lizzie gripped his hand tighter around her and whispered,

"Stay," deliberately pressing her bottom up against his aroused member.

The urge to flip her over and crawl back on top of her was strong, but there was an even more overwhelming urge to run. Panic set its spurs in hardest as a hollow darkness created a pit in his stomach.

"I have to go," he said, louder than he should have.

Lizzie released his hand quickly this time and allowed him to slide out of bed uninterrupted. He dressed quickly, tucking his annoyingly aroused member back into his breeches.

"What's wrong, Rupert?" Lizzie asked quietly, sitting up in bed and pulling the sheet up to cover her breasts.

"Nothing at all," Rupert lied, unable to look at her.

He moved over to the mirror and quickly tied his cravat and waistcoat. He had done this a hundred times before. Why were his hands shaking so much?

"Why don't you climb back into bed? It's still early." Lizzie tried once more, her voice soft and non-threatening.

Rupert had the strangest urge to laugh. If he was honest with himself, he wanted nothing more than to turn around and climb back into her bed. And stay there, wrapped in her embrace. Perhaps forever.

Why did she have to do this to him? He had been perfectly happy living his rakehell life. Well maybe he had been getting a little bored with it, but even so. Why did she have to come along and confuse him when he wasn't ready? He wasn't thirty yet! He had more time.

So, as he always did when he was pushed past his limits into uncomfortable territory, he lost his temper and lashed out.

"Lizzie, please stop nagging at me. You are not my wife. We had a splendid time last night, but I need to get back to my house. We'll meet again soon." As soon as the words were out of his mouth he regretted them, but it was too late.

Lizzie gasped and then nodded, her brows coming together in a scowl.

"I'm sure you know the way out," she said stiffly, her pain-drenched brown eyes flashing before she turned away and presented him with her back.

Rupert felt her hurt and shame as though it were his own. It choked him, especially knowing he was the cause. He spent one more moment looking at her, just to torture himself, before he silently grabbed his coat and walked out.

Two weeks later, Rupert found John exercising at their boxing club. The two friends enjoyed the physicality of the sport; the sweat. It was very ungentlemanly, but that didn't stop them. The physical benefits were evident also, another thing they both enjoyed.

Rupert stood for a moment, watching John with an opponent. John was very graceful and controlled. He reminded Rupert of Archie sometimes, despite their other differences. The bell rang, and John stopped, shook hands with his opponent and walked out of the boxing area.

"Rupert," he huffed, pleased to see his friend.

"John," Rupert greeted his only unmarried friend. Sometimes he felt that Oliver and Archie had an affinity because of their wives and that he and John had been left in open space. But they had each other, which was comforting.

"Come have a whiskey with me?" John suggested, pulling his jacket on. The boxing club had a small drinking area for its members to unwind and to get to know each other.

Rupert hesitated for one moment. He needed to hit

something. Then again, whiskey was like water to him. He could box after they had a drink.

"I haven't seen you for a few weeks," John said casually, taking a long swig of the best whiskey the club offered, which wasn't anywhere near the standard Rupert and John usually drank.

Grimacing at the burn, Rupert answered with a shrug.

"Just been busy."

"New mistress?" John asked with a lopsided smile.

Rupert frowned. He only wished that was the reason he had been off the circuit.

"I have been visiting a new lady recently, but I don't think it'll be a permanent thing." Rupert breathed unevenly, hoping he was lying. He couldn't talk to John about Lizzie. He simply couldn't.

"No loss, I'm sure. There's always another one waiting to fill the position, isn't there?" John laughed out loud at his joke.

Rupert tried to smile but didn't quite manage it. John was correct about one thing—there were always other women waiting. He was always inundated with calling cards and letters.

The problem was, Rupert wasn't sure anymore if he wanted anyone other than Lizzie.

"You?" Rupert asked, trying to deflect the attention away from himself.

John smiled, although it did not reach his eyes.

"I'm currently moving my latest out, and the new one goes in next week." He spoke as though he was exchanging horses. It was a conversation that had never bothered him before, but for some reason today, it made him uncomfortable.

"Six months up?" He tried to joke, knowing that John had a rule that no mistress lasted longer than six months. It must have cost him a fortune to pay them off, but then again, John had money. They all did.

"Not even. Four." John laughed, shaking his head.

"What was wrong with her? Or do I not want to know?"

"The stupid wench started talking about the long term, babies and such." John huffed in disgust and smacked his palm down onto the table.

Uh-oh, Rupert thought. The poor woman had broken John's ultimate rule.

"Oliver and Archie seem happy, don't they?" Rupert muttered, once John had finished making noises.

John looked up in obvious alarm.

"We're not going to talk about them, are we?" he gasped.

"Why ever not?" Rupert asked, honestly surprised by the horrified look on his friend's face. The four of them had been friends since they were thirteen-years-old.

"Because they're married now. They've changed."

Rupert blinked, not sure how to answer that. They had changed, it was true, but Rupert thought it was for the better.

"So, if I got married you wouldn't want to see me anymore?" Rupert asked John lightly, smiling as though it were all a joke.

"It's not that, they are just so goddamn happy, I'm sick of it. If you got married, you wouldn't turn into them." John raised his glass of whiskey. The implication made Rupert feel sick.

Was that really how John saw him? As a man incapable of loving his wife, or of being faithful to her? "Did you see the new figures on the exchange this morning?" Rupert asked, changing the subject abruptly. He couldn't talk about the subject of women, relationships or marriage anymore.

All he could think about was how he had left things with Lizzie, and how his inadequacies had made themselves known.

He was utterly exhausted.

Chapter 12

Three weeks later, Lizzie was at her wit's end.

Two weeks ago, she had met Viscount Courtney at a small private ball. He had quickly shown interest in Lizzie, and she had encouraged him. Not knowing where she stood with Rupert since he had stormed out of her bedchamber in a huff, she had decided to encourage the attentions of this new and eligible suitor.

Viscount Courtney was a rather nice-looking gentleman. He had cropped brown hair and brown eyes. He was taller than Lizzie but was no imposing figure. He liked to read and manage his profitable estate. He had come to town specifically to find a wife. A wife who wanted to move to the country and who wanted to continue his family's tradition of having at least six children.

Lizzie went for two private walks and a ride with the viscount. He had also called on her at home several times and had danced with her at several balls. He was pleasant and quiet. He was everything she had originally set out to find. He didn't need a dowry and was happy to court her, an older widow, rather than go straight for an eighteen-year-old debutante.

Whilst on a walk the day before he had proposed marriage between them—a marriage based on mutual interests and respect. However, instead of accepting with alacrity as she had fully expected to should he ask, she had wanted to bring up her breakfast on his shoes. She had prevaricated and not given him an answer yet, although she had promised one in the next few days.

Lizzie was so confused about her own feelings that she had finally decided to do something about it. She really couldn't stay in this limbo state any longer and knew she had to either convince Rupert to marry her or put him aside forever.

Since she hadn't seen Rupert in a while, she needed to know where they stood. Rupert hadn't contacted her, but he also hadn't been at any of the balls, luncheons or dinners she had attended. He had simply disappeared, and Lizzie was too proud to ask Charlotte or any of her other connections where he might be.

Lizzie missed him dreadfully, and if she was going to make her life with someone else, then she needed to close the door on Rupert first. Everything still felt so unfinished, and as though her heart had a great big, gaping hole in it. It was a horrible feeling and not one she had ever expected to experience.

She had accidentally learned from Charlotte this morning that Rupert was attending the soirée Lizzie was also attending tonight. She couldn't wait. She was determined to find out what was happening with Mr. Rupert Willoughby once and for all.

When she arrived at Lady Melbourne's house party, Lizzie's body was humming with anticipation. After taking off her drawers at the very last minute before leaving the house, she felt positively naked. She was so aware of that part of herself that wanted Rupert so much that she kept clenching those internal muscles. It was horribly uncomfortable to be so aroused with no relief in sight.

Lizzie stood in a small circle of people, trying to discreetly look around the room. She couldn't see Rupert. Was he in the card room with some of the other men? Or was he off with one of his many women? The thought made her frown and her heart ache in a rather painful sort of way.

"He's in the music room I believe, Lizzie," Charlotte murmured into her ear so that no one else could hear.

Lizzie flushed guiltily but gave Charlotte a grateful smile.

"Excuse me." She curtseyed to their group and made her way along the hallway to the music room. She hadn't seen Rupert since the morning he had left her room.

"Would you please get off me, Elise?" Rupert's voice came through the open music room door, loud and annoyed.

Lizzie stalled outside the door, not sure whether she should retreat or burst in on them. She had no right to interrupt, as she wasn't his wife. So, she stayed still and listened.

"I heard your latest mistress has gone. Why don't you take me home instead?" The woman purred.

"Because I am not interested in you or what you are offering. I told you I am not available." Rupert's syllables were clipped, and Lizzie could hear the restrained anger in his tone.

"But I know what you like. I could…" the woman purred again.

Lizzie almost gagged.

"I don't care what you think you know, I'm not the same person I was a month ago. I don't want a mistress any longer." Rupert spoke slowly and succinctly as though he were talking to a child.

Dead silence.

"You plan on *marrying*?" The incredulous voice sounded almost wounded.

"At some stage, yes, Of course, I do," Rupert said, quieter now.

"Then you can play until then," the woman said, her voice oozing honey.

Lizzie tried not to smile; obviously, the woman was married, or she'd be trying to talk him into marrying her instead.

"Elise, listen to me. It is over between us. Stop."

The command in the words was unmistakable, and Lizzie decided this was the time to enter. She may not get another opening.

She walked through the door, trying to look as though she hadn't been listening.

"Oh, good evening," she greeted them both with a polite and falsely surprised smile.

"My lord," she then greeted Rupert directly, curtseying lower than was necessary.

Rupert gave Elise a look that clearly told her to leave.

The blonde looked ready to commit murder. She stared between Rupert and Lizzie and her eyes narrowed.

"Are you telling me that this little mouse has you under her spell? You couldn't possibly want *her*." Elise pointed at Lizzie and all but spat the words.

Rupert gave Lizzie all his attention, and didn't even glance back at the blonde.

"Please leave us," he said, rudely flicking his wrist toward the entrance of the room. The woman stormed out and Lizzie couldn't help the smile that lifted her lips. Rupert followed Elise quickly, closing the door and sliding the lock into place.

Her pulse quickened as he turned back to her. Just seeing him after all this time was a powerful aphrodisiac. He seemed to feel the same way, if the greedy look in his eyes was any indication.

"God, you're beautiful, Lizzie. I've missed you."

"I've been here. Where have you been?" she demanded. Lizzie had originally assumed that Rupert had moved on from her. But after hearing his conversation with Elise, she was almost certain he hadn't.

"At home, at my club, nowhere special." Rupert shrugged, moving back to stand by the fireplace.

"Really? Haven't been interviewing new mistresses?" Lizzie couldn't resist asking.

"No, I told you I don't want anyone but you," Rupert said, the aloof mask falling from his face and showing her how much he meant what he said.

She gasped at the raw emotion on his face, but clenched her teeth against her growing need. First, she wanted answers.

"You still feel that way? I thought after you left my bed so abruptly three weeks ago and never came back that you had decided I didn't quite fill the position." Lizzie allowed her hurt to show. Her eyes shimmered with tears at the remembered pain but she blinked them back before they could fall.

"I'm sorry if I made you feel that way. I had no plans to be with anyone else." he admitted

"Then why did you leave like that?" Lizzie asked the question she had waited three weeks to know.

"Because I wasn't sure if I was ready for a commitment that included waking up next to you," Rupert admitted gruffly. "Why was it so horrible?" Lizzie asked, choking on the words. She'd never woken up in the arms of a man. Her husband had always slept in his own bed following intercourse. "No, that was the problem. It felt good and reasonable.., and like something I could do every day of my life." Rupert admitted. "When I woke with you in my arms, everything felt so right that it scared me. It scared me so much I ran. I'm not proud of how I handled things that morning. But that's the truth, Lizzie."

"Why were you so scared? What was the problem?" Lizzie asked, exasperated now. He truly was like a five-year-old in a twenty-eight-year-old body.

"The problem is that I have never spent the night with anyone before!" Rupert barked.

"Never?" Lizzie repeated, shocked. Hadn't he slept next to all of his mistresses?

"Never. Waking up with you in my arms and your soft body curved against mine..." Rupert's hands curled as though still holding her.

"Tell me," Lizzie whispered, desperate for some clarity.

"I can't explain it to you. I had to leave, but I didn't mean to hurt you." Rupert answered gruffly. Lizzie sighed heavily, disappointed with his response. It was clear that he felt something for her beyond physical, but why could he not admit that? She was half in love with the big oaf, and he was running scared from his feelings for her. How was she ever going to truly know how he felt? How was she going to tell him that she was considering marrying someone who was the Anti-Rupert?

Easily, she realised. Just open your mouth and tell him.

"Viscount Courtney proposed to me yesterday," she announced, biting the metaphorical bullet. She strolled, pretending casualness, over to the piano and sat down on the stool.

If she wanted a test of Rupert's feelings, then this would certainly be it.

"Has he indeed?" Rupert said, stilling suddenly. "And what answer did you give him?" When she glanced up at him, Rupert's face was studiously blank.

"I haven't yet given him an answer. He is offering me everything I thought I wanted. He is a gentleman who spends most of his time on his country estate. He comes from a large family and intends to continue the tradition," Lizzie explained, blushing. It felt very strange discussing marrying, and therefore procreating with another man, when you were talking to your lover.

"You can't marry him," Rupert exploded.

"Why not?" Lizzie asked quietly. She looked up at him with eyes that begged him to give her a reason, any reason.

She was so confused. She had finally achieved exactly what she had thought she wanted. A polite, quiet gentleman had offered her marriage and family.

And yet she was no longer sure if she still wanted that calm, average existence she had once believed to be the pinnacle of achievement.

"Because...because..." Rupert floundered, throwing his arms around. He looked like the epitome of a ruffled gentleman.

Why not indeed. Lizzie studied him with a frown. A respectable, rather dull, but nice gentleman was offering her exactly what she wanted, but what Rupert himself refused to offer. Obviously, he wasn't sure he could offer her marriage, but he didn't want her marrying someone else?

Annoyance rose in Lizzie's breast.

"Because *why*, Rupert? You need to give me a proper reason," she persisted. She knew Rupert cared for her, but how *much* did he care? As much as he had for every other lover he had taken? More? Enough to offer for her? Or just enough to not want to stop bedding her quite yet?

"Because I still want you," he said. "I thought you were enjoying our... this." He gestured between them. "I've never spent the night with a woman sleeping in his arms before you, Lizzie," he said again, as if that explained everything.

She smiled sadly.

"I *am* enjoying this," she gestured in the replica of his hand movement. "Although I wasn't sure after what happened three weeks ago that we were still..." she trailed off and did the gesture again. "I haven't seen or heard from you since then."

"Of course, we are. I'm so sorry I hurt you." Rupert apologised again. "I shouldn't have left it so long to contact you again."

"Please keep enjoying it—enjoying us," Rupert whispered, pulling her into his arms and bending to kiss her lips.

Lizzie pushed at his chest and kept him from kissing her.

"Are you suggesting I continue bedding you *and* my new husband?" she asked, shocked to the core. Did she mean so little to him? Did he think her that disloyal that she would treat either him or the viscount in such a disrespectful manner? Did he not mind the idea of sharing her? She had wanted to kill that piece of trash that had accosted Rupert here a few minutes earlier.

Rupert's eyes darkened, and his hold on her arms became almost painful.

"Never," he growled, barely speaking the syllables. His hold tightened further, and Lizzie gasped.

She saw the clouds of a storm rolling in across his features. It was clear now that Rupert had a temper, and the very idea of Lizzie bedding another man seemed to be causing it to rear up.

She felt both dismayed and excited by the knowledge that she could create such passion in the man in front of her.

"You are mine," he growled again, sweeping his hands beneath her skirts and lifting her up on to the pianoforte. He pushed her body down to make her lay flat and flipped her skirts up to her waist.

He let out a gasp when he discovered she was naked beneath her skirts.

Rupert moaned his pleasure at seeing her sex laid out before him, so ready for his touch. He remembered once asking her if she would come to a ball naked beneath her skirts for him. He had never even considered the idea that she might do as he asked. The idea that she had only him in her mind, and not this new man, drove his need higher than it had ever been.

He forced her thighs wide and opened her to his gaze. She was beautiful even here. Light pink and soft, and Lord help him, already wet for him. Unable to resist, he pressed his thumb deep into her passage without warning, to prove to them both how ready she was. She arched her back, and opened her mouth on a moan.

"Rupert," she begged, trembling hard. "I need you. I want you to *possess* me."

He wanted more than that. He wanted to mark her, to show her and everyone else that she was taken. That she was his.

He wanted her so much..

"Take me, please," she moaned, gripping his thumb with her inner muscles.

Rupert groaned and watched her writhe in pleasure. Her fingers clenched his hand where it lay on her belly, holding her down. He removed his thumb and took both of her hands in his, interlinking their fingers. Lizzie looked up at him then, and Rupert could see her need. His heart jolted in realisation.

I love this woman.

Desperate for Rupert to possess her, Lizzie writhed beneath his touch. He held her thighs open wide, still gripping her hands with his. He looked down at her beautiful flesh, knelt on the ground and buried his face between her legs.

That first press of lips on her most sensitive flesh made her scream. She didn't care anymore whether someone might hear. She could only focus on the pleasure that Rupert delivered between her legs. Rupert didn't stop at her scream. He ran his tongue around her swelling flesh and down the crevice, before thrusting his tongue into her over and over again. She cried out her pleasure in time with his tongue thrusts. She tried desperately to sit up and reach him, but Rupert held her ruthlessly down. He returned to the flesh of her swollen bud and suckled, stronger and stronger, and her pleasure grew and grew until she could contain herself no longer. She cried out her orgasm, her body convulsing over and over again beneath his mouth.

Spent from the most intense moment of her life, she lay limp and helpless, but Rupert wasn't done with her. He got to his feet with a surge and ripped open his breeches. His erection sprang proudly forth, huge and purple.

"You're mine," he growled, guiding his manhood to her dripping entrance and setting the head at the opening.

"Say it, Lizzie," he demanded, not giving her body what it craved most. "Say you're mine."

Lizzie wrapped her legs around his buttocks and tried to pull him inside her. He held perfectly still and stared down at her.

Lizzie looked up and saw the blue eyes she knew so well. Tonight, they were almost black. He was on the verge of something quite life-altering, she could feel it.

"Make me," she whispered, wriggling her hips so that she got some pleasure from the position, despite his statue-like stance.

A growl filled the air around her as he seemed to lose all control; all gentlemanly concern for her as a delicate lady. He grasped her hips tightly in both hands and thrust hard, so deep he knocked on her womb in one push. Then he pulled back and thrust as deeply again. And again. This was no slow burn of mutual pleasure, no gentle persuasion. This was possession, and it called her to respond despite the violence.

Rupert didn't hold back, pounding into her small body with a force that threatened to break her. She didn't care. She was lost. She could feel nothing but a continuous pressure, filling her, changing her, demanding that she tell him that she was his and his alone.

"Yes," she answered the silent question his body was asking.

"Say it. Say you're mine," Rupert demanded, unrelenting in his hammering.

Lizzie felt it building faster than it ever had. She was going to scream again.

As if Rupert felt her tighten he slowed to almost no movement. He pulled out and pushed back in, slowly, gradually.

Lizzie groaned. How could he do that to her? She didn't want care, she wanted him as he had been a moment ago. No finesse, just pure need.

She looked up and saw the set face, the tightened jaw and the blue eyes that were glittering mutiny. Lizzie would declare herself or he wouldn't release her from this sensual torment.

"I'm yours," she whispered. "Yours, Rupert.".

• • •

Rupert shouted in triumph and picked up the pace.

"Only mine," he demanded.

"Yes, only yours," she agreed, moaning and arching her back as he started to move as fast and hard as he had before.

She screamed out loud and arched her back as she came, and Rupert kept thrusting through her orgasm and beyond. She quivered in every muscle before collapsing heavily, her eyes closing.

Rupert wouldn't have that. He bent down and captured her mouth, devouring her essence; her taste. He thrust his tongue into her as possessively from above as he was below. His release was imminent. He had barely managed to survive her declaration and her unbelievable orgasm. Now that she was face to face with him, looking into his eyes and holding him tightly, he knew he was gone.

He swelled within her, an answering groan pulled from her lips. He started to withdraw and something strange happened. "No," she demanded, beneath him, tightening her sheath around him.

Rupert felt his release descend, and he tried to push back from Lizzie to spill himself upon his handkerchief, but he couldn't pull away. Lizzie had dug her heels into his buttocks, and her arms pulled him closer. He looked into her face, desperate. It was going to be too late.

"You're mine too," she declared, her sheath caressing his organ.

And his release started. He buried his head in her neck and cried out. His cock thrust up to the hilt and his seed spilled into her body while he enjoyed the full caress of her slick walls. Nothing had ever felt so good—he thought he might faint from the pleasure. He slumped against her, completely drained, and she held him tighter. Stroking his hair, she murmured again, "You're mine too."

He sobbed and pulled abruptly out of her body and away from her. Fumbling with his open breeches, he stumbled to the door.

Lizzie's skirts fell back into place as she gingerly slid off the pianoforte. "Are you okay?" she asked with genuine concern in her voice. Rupert felt as though he was being tortured. He was terrified at what was happening. He had never felt this way, ever, in his life.

"I have to go, I'm sorry," he apologised, unable to see any other way of dealing with the overwhelming emotions that flowed through his body and mind.

"Okay, if you must," Lizzie murmured.

Rupert looked over his shoulder once as he opened the door. Regret filled him at the confused look in her expression.

"I didn't hurt you, did I?" He asked gruffly, running a hand through his dishevelled hair.

Lizzie shook her head emphatically. "Physically? No."

But her feelings were once again hurt. He could tell by the sadness in her beautiful eyes.

I love you, he wanted to shout. But he was too afraid.

Instead, he simply stared at the woman he loved and then ran from the room.

What was he going to do? He had experienced the most incredible joining of his life that went far beyond the physical realm. Could he marry a woman like Lizzie? A woman who would expect fidelity? A woman who would expect children? Hell, he may have just given her a child. He heard her declaration ringing in his ears as he pounded out the front door and called for his carriage.

You're mine too!

Chapter 13

"Lizzie, it is so good to see you!" Charlotte exclaimed, seated on her chaise in the middle of the formal sitting room. "Forgive me for not getting up, my back has been ever so sore." She smiled serenely and rubbed her large belly.

Lizzie curtseyed and sat down opposite her friend. Her envy of Charlotte's condition made her heart ache, and she had to swallow against the unwanted tears.

"Don't be silly. You're splendid for seeing me at all. If you were like our mothers, you would stay reclined on the chaise for the next three months," Lizzie joked, attempting to ease her own discomfort with humour.

Charlotte chuckled, and Lizzie smiled. When was the last time that had happened?

"What brings you to visit, Lizzie? Would you like a cup of tea? Do you have something on your mind?" Charlotte asked, cocking her head to one side.

Lizzie grimaced. How did this person know her so well? Was her broken heart status so clearly written on her forehead?

Charlotte and Lizzie's mothers had been childhood friends, and she'd seen Charlotte throughout their lives. She was a kind, fiery, beautiful lady, who Lizzie admired greatly.

"I've come to say goodbye, dear Charlotte. I've decided to go home," Lizzie explained, trying her best to sound cheerful.

She was running away, and that didn't sit well with her. But she could see no other way. She'd refused Viscount Courtney on principle, and now that she'd lost Rupert, her heart was broken.

"But the Season isn't even half finished, Lizzie. I thought you were hoping to remarry this year?" Charlotte asked, her tone puzzled.

"I...ah..." Lizzie's prepared speech stuck in her throat, and she looked down at her hands clasped in her lap.

Lizzie heard the swish of silk skirts as Charlotte made her way over to her side.

"Tell me what's happened," Charlotte probed, sitting down next to Lizzie and sliding her hand into hers.

Heat tingled in the back of her throat and moved up into her eyes.

"It's Rupert," Lizzie sobbed, unable to hold back her tears anymore. She hadn't been able to discuss this with anyone and the weight of it was hurting her.

Charlotte inhaled sharply and opened her mouth wide. "Archie," she screamed.

Lizzie covered her ears. She'd never heard a lady scream before.

At least, other than her own screams when Rupert pleasured her so intensely.

"No, no, you can't tell him anything." Lizzie grabbed her friend's hands, shocked that Charlotte would betray a confidence. Why would she be calling for her husband?

Charlotte frowned. "I'm sorry, Lizzie, but if you want to know why Rupert has done something, or how he feels, then you have to ask someone who knows him. My husband has been friends with that scoundrel for almost twenty years, and if anyone can give you an insight into Rupert Willoughby, it's Archie." Charlotte nodded once and finished her speech with a smug smile.

"He's not a scoundrel," Lizzie whispered, a tear sliding down her cheek.

"You called, my dear?" came an amused voice from the door.

Lizzie looked up and gave Archie a thin smile. His smile was cordial and not the least bit angry that he had been summoned in such a way. Lizzie didn't think any gentleman should be subject to this sort of questioning. But Charlotte was right. Lizzie wanted answers, not just a shoulder to cry on.

Archibald Turner, the future Marquis of Hunting and the current Earl of Tother, inclined his head. Instead of running away as Lizzie expected him to do, he instructed the butler that they weren't to be disturbed, stepped into the room and shut the door.

Charlotte's husband was very handsome, but quite serious. He was much leaner in build compared to Rupert. His eyes were gentle and his attire that Lizzie so often found overwhelming, was quite dull today. For some reason, Lizzie found that comforting.

"How can I help?" Archie asked, sitting down opposite them.

He showed little emotion on his face, but Lizzie saw kindness in his eyes.

"Tell him," Charlotte urged Lizzie. The command in her voice was unmistakable.

Lizzie glared at her friend. What did Charlotte expect her to say? That Rupert had given her the most incredible pleasure of her life and then ran away when things became too serious between them?

Never. She wasn't even sure she could articulate the words. She shook her head and refused to open her mouth.

"Rupert seduced her, and now he's ignoring her," Charlotte announced.

Lizzie gasped. "He didn't seduce me."

"But he did take you to his bed?" Charlotte prodded.

"Yes," Lizzie whispered although it had never been in his bed. She looked down again, hanging her head.

"How often? If you don't mind me asking." Archie's voice came quietly through the silence.

Lizzie sighed. If she ran away to her country estate, she would never know why the man she loved had run from her. Archie was the best person to ask. But how did one guess what was in another's heart?

How could she divulge what had happened between them the last time they were together? It would be too embarrassing.

"Three different days, several times," Lizzie answered, heat racing up her neck and flourishing over her face like the fire crackling in the grate.

Archie cleared his throat. "I'm sorry to say, that isn't unusual. Rupert has always shared a woman's bed for as long as they were both agreeable and then moved on. I'm sorry," Archie apologised, clearing his throat yet again.

He was clearly uncomfortable, shuffling on the chaise and

glancing to the ground when she looked at him. However, at the behest of his wife he was doing his best to help. For this, she would love Archie and Charlotte forever.

"You don't have to apologise. I know he's a rake." Lizzie picked at the white lace on her waistband.

"Then how can I help you?" Archie asked, looking between them with his eyes wide, clearly baffled as to why he had been dragged into this awkward conversation.

Lizzie received a sharp jab in the thigh from Charlotte and looked at her, startled.

"Ask him. If you want to know something, ask."

Her bright smile gave Lizzie confidence, and she blushed again as she readied herself for the conversation to come. This went against every rule that she had ever been taught about polite society. Then again, Archie and Charlotte were aristocracy. If they sanctioned such talk, could it be so bad?

"I was wondering why I scared him so much," Lizzie explained, clenching her skirts in her hands.

"I don't understand what you mean," Archie asked, gently again.

"Well, the first time was relatively normal. The second time he stayed overnight at my house and said he got scared because it felt good to wake up with me and…"

Archie's swift intake of breath stopped her mid-sentence.

"He stayed the night with you? Slept…with you?" he asked, his eyes wide.

"Yes," Lizzie admitted, blushing again at Archie's direct look. Why was that so unbelievable?

"Why is that so shocking?" Charlotte asked, echoing Lizzie's thoughts. She was apparently confused as to why Archie had stopped Lizzie at that point in her story.

Archie shifted in his seat and cleared his throat again.

"Rupert never sleeps the night with anyone. He doesn't like to establish any intimacy."

Charlotte made an unladylike scoffing sound and Archie hushed her.

"Charlotte, there's a big difference for a man between the physical bedding activity and real intimacy. That's why most men go to brothels, because they can leave immediately afterwards. It's what separates the whores from wives or true lovers," Archie explained, more emotion in his voice than Lizzie had ever heard before.

"Not that you'd know," Charlotte reminded him with a smug smile.

"Not that I'd know," Archie returned, giving Charlotte a smile of such sweetness that Lizzie had to look away for fear of crying again. Why couldn't Rupert love her like that?

"So, the fact that he spent the night with you means something, Mrs. Symmons," Archie explained quietly, speaking the words slowly as though they were a foreign language.

"Oh, it's Lizzie," she exclaimed, amazed that she had never given Archie leave to use her first name.

"Thank you, and please call me Archie." He smiled warmly, and Lizzie smiled back.

"So, explain to me why he got so upset that morning and ran out," Lizzie asked again, shuffling to the edge of her seat. It still didn't make sense to her.

Archie smiled sadly. "I can't tell you exactly why, but I know that Rupert has spent the last ten years making sure that no woman has meant anything to him. Every woman he has been with has been disposable."

"He told me he wants no one else except me," Lizzie whispered, a tear escaping her eye at the memory. She dashed it away with the back of her hand.

Archie stilled as both ladies turned to look at his shocked expression. He cleared his throat and then coughed loudly.

"Then that would be a first," he said, obviously trying not to say too much.

"And there's one more thing, but I'm not sure I can say it," Lizzie announced quietly, jiggling in the excitement of revelation. What she was about to say was beyond inexcusable.

But she was bursting with it, and the news would erupt soon enough.

"You can tell us anything," Charlotte encouraged, patting Lizzie's knee again.

Lizzie took a deep breath, amazed she was even considering this.

"Well, last week when we were together, he made me say I was his and only his, so that I wouldn't marry Viscount Courtney," Lizzie confided. This was something that she knew she shouldn't share, but it seemed important somehow.

"Holy God," Archie breathed, looking more shocked by the minute. He was blinking rapidly, and his eyebrows had risen on his forehead.

"And there's one more thing, but I'm very embarrassed to admit it," Lizzie murmured. She was totally committed now; there was no holding back. She took a deep breath and told them. "The real reason I want to leave is that I'm afraid he won't forgive me for what I did to him. I can't handle seeing him with other women. It would break my heart."

"What could you have done to him?" Charlotte asked, looking between Lizzie and Archie as though the answer could be found there.

"Well, he has always, well, not finished inside..." Lizzie trailed off, mortified, but determined to finish. She looked down at her lap, then snuck a peek at Archie.

Archie blushed but nodded in understanding.

"But last week, well, he'd said I was his and I only wanted to prove he was mine too and I wouldn't let him pull away," Lizzie blurted out in a rush.

Lizzie looked at her friend and found that Charlotte had her mouth hanging open. Lizzie had an overwhelming urge to laugh. To confound Lady Charlotte, future marchioness and daughter of a dragon dowager duchess, was a remarkable thing.

Archie stood and paced, growing more agitated and more restless with each step. He murmured to himself, flinging his hands behind him and then forward again.

Lizzie opened her mouth to speak, but he held up his hand to stop her.

"Could you let me think, please?" And without waiting for a response, he continued pacing.

He continued for a full minute, the longest of Lizzie's life. Then he sat down again with exuberance.

"This is incredible," he breathed, his eyes bright.

Lizzie looked over at Charlotte to see a rather warm expression building in her friend's face. She obviously enjoyed seeing her husband look so excited. Even Lizzie had to admit that Archie was rather handsome when he was smiling. He should do it more often.

"Why?" Lizzie exclaimed, dragging her wandering mind back to the conversation. "Why is it incredible, and why would it cause him to run out on me?" she asked, frustrated to the extreme.

Archie laughed hysterically, then sobered quickly.

"I apologise." He bobbed his head in a half-bow.

Lizzie waited with drawn breath.

"Rupert never does that. Ever!" he stated, letting out the breath he had been holding.

"Okay, so he doesn't do that. Why is it such a big issue?" Lizzie asked, still not understanding the problem.

Archie laughed again, a beautiful, rich sound.

"Rupert has a severe issue with producing illegitimate children. His brother has two and favours them over his legitimate daughters. Rupert has always done everything he can not to produce children with his mistresses," Archie explained, still excited at this discovery.

"I don't think it's going to be a problem. I didn't conceive after eleven months of marriage," Lizzie murmured unthinkingly, then swallowed hard.

"It only takes once," Charlotte said, a laugh hidden in her voice.

Archie smiled again, this time giving his wife an indulgent smile and Lizzie found herself wondering how Charlotte's marriage had started.

"So, he's upset with me because he might have sired a child?" Lizzie asked. Her brows were knitting together in confusion. If that was the problem, then she was hugely disappointed in Rupert.

"No. That he even did it at all, is the problem. Rupert has always had control of his affairs and his body. He told me once that he had never even been tempted to stay inside a woman past a certain point. And you have to realise that you didn't make him, he's twice as strong as you. If he wanted to leave you, you wouldn't have been able to stop him," Archie explained, giving Lizzie a kind smile.

"So, he wanted to stay with me?" Lizzie asked, bewildered. She had been berating herself for the past week for holding on to him. It had never occurred to her until this moment that a man like Rupert could pull away if he wanted to.

"Yes, I think he did, and that for Rupert would be a problem," Archie explained again, giving Charlotte a pointed look.

"I still don't understand." Lizzie sighed, twirling her wedding ring around her right ring finger where she had moved it when she'd come to London to re-marry.

"Rupert hates that he will one day have to marry to secure his brother's heir. He never wanted that responsibility and has avoided love at all costs. You have surprised him, and he is terrified that you are making him want things he has avoided for so long," Archie murmured.

It was probably the most words she had ever heard the earl say.

"So, he cares about me," Lizzie concluded quietly, speaking more to herself than anyone else.

"Yes, I believe so," Archie agreed just as softly.

"I thought he did. I don't know why that was so wrong," Lizzie said, voicing the sadness she had been feeling since that day in the music room. Why was it so terrible for them to care for one another? Rupert had to marry at some stage, and she wanted to marry him. Why was he running away from a relationship that would be filled with passion and mutual affection?

"It isn't wrong. Rupert is readjusting his whole outlook on life and that is apparently causing him problems." Archie shrugged, accompanying it with a wry smile that conveyed an understanding of where Rupert was at presently.

"Thank you." Lizzie smiled, despite the fresh tears she could feel tingling in her eyes. She felt better. She didn't understand fully, but her problem was shared and therefore it had been halved.

"Now, my dear, may I go back to my study?" Archie faced Charlotte, giving her a mock scowl and a bow.

"Yes, and thank you, my love." Charlotte smiled up at her husband.

Archie stepped closer to his wife and dropped his voice to a whisper.

"Are you feeling well?" he asked.

Lizzie had the feeling that if she weren't there, Archie would have touched Charlotte. He was obviously restraining himself.

Charlotte nodded, rubbing her belly happily again.

Archie's eyes lingered on Charlotte for a moment longer and then he bowed to them both and left the room.

"So, what exactly does all of that mean?" Lizzie asked, turning expectant eyes on Charlotte. She wanted to understand better. Perhaps Charlotte could interpret everything that Archie had said.

Charlotte chewed her lip a moment, puzzled.

"I think that means that Rupert cares for you," she announced slowly.

"I thought so, but why is that such a big deal?" Lizzie asked, still no closer to understanding why Rupert had such an issue caring about her.

Charlotte began laughing and kept laughing, holding her belly on either side to contain the ripples of movement.

They both heard the front door close and turned toward it.

"Who do you think that is?" Lizzie asked.

"Doesn't matter, the butler will turn them away," Charlotte reassured Lizzie with a flick of her hand. Like most people of her class, Charlotte had servants milling around her since the day she was born. She trusted them to do as she asked, no questions asked.

"So why did you laugh?" Lizzie asked quietly, wondering why something that was so devastating to her could be so humorous to somebody else.

"You have to understand how I see Rupert, Lizzie. He has always been the *ton's* foremost rake. Handsome, charming and ruthless in his relationships. He has a permanent mistress and dallies with any woman who wants him."

Lizzie frowned at the reminder of who Rupert was, but Charlotte continued regardless.

"And now the rake is no more. He wants you and only you, and I just love it."

"But he doesn't want me, or he wouldn't be hiding."

Charlotte laughed again. "Of course, he does; that's *why* he is hiding. I will give him one month to come to his senses and ask you to marry him. Otherwise, I will find you a husband myself."

Charlotte grinned, and Lizzie couldn't help the small flutters of hope coming to life beneath her breast. She could only hope that he did want her, because now that she knew for sure it was he that she wanted, no one else would do.

Chapter 14

As though a judge was in his ear, Rupert could hear the man speaking, adjudicating his life. *Here sits Lord Rupert Willoughby, heir to the Earl of Sweeting, drinking alone.*

How miserable.

"Rupert." Archie's voice greeted him moments before his friend sat down opposite him.

Rupert grabbed his port glass and squeezed the crystal, staring into the depths of the red liqueur. He did not want to see his perpetually happy friend. Archie may be reserved, but his happiness radiated like a lone star at night.

He was not in the mood for any luminescent good moods.

"Archie, you know I love you and Charlotte, but you do not want to be around me today."

"Why ever not?" Archie asked, calling for more port.

Rupert groaned and shifted irritably in his seat. Why couldn't he just be left alone to be miserable? He should never have left his house.

"Don't you have a pregnant wife to watch over?" Rupert asked, unable to get the image of his hands around Charlotte's swollen belly out of his mind. That moment had rocked the foundations of his world. A condition that he had always considered a necessary evil now took on the guise of something beautiful, sensual even.

"She has company today," Archie said lightly, taking a sip of the golden liquor.

"Who?" Rupert looked up at his friend's strangely smug expression, suspicion burning in his gut. Archie had not found him by accident.

"Lizzie," Archie announced with a knowing smile, taking another small sip of his drink.

Rupert groaned and put his head down on the table with a large thud.

"Are you going to stay there?" Archie asked, amusement obvious in his jovial tones.

Yes, forever.

"Did you know that out of the four spares, John's the only one to be still considered as such," Archie said calmly.

"The Spares" was what the group of their four friends had been referred to. They were all born the spare sons of wealthy, titled, old aristocratic families. Oliver had inherited after his brother and father had died. Archie was his father's heir now that his older brother had passed and Rupert was his brother's heir after the latter had failed to produce a son.

Rupert groaned at the reminder but lifted his head and thrust a lock of black hair off his forehead.

"And if John's sister-in-law fails to have a son, then he'll inherit too," Rupert laughed humourlessly. Amazing. How the mighty had fallen.

Archie nodded silently and took another sip of his port. "That is true."

Rupert stared at his friend. Archie had obviously come to tell him something, so why didn't he get on with it?

When his solemn friend said nothing more, Rupert clenched his fists and brought them both down onto the table in front of him, hard. There was no one else in the room, and he glared openly at Archie.

"Are you going to tell me how Lizzie is, or did you mention her to torture me?" Rupert asked angrily.

Archie's eyes narrowed, but Rupert could still see the humour in them, and it made his belly tighten.

"Well?" he repeated through clenched teeth.

"She's well," Archie answered with a smile.

"Well? She's bloody *well*?" Rupert repeated. How could she be well when he was confused and lost, and so many other horrible emotions he had never experienced before that made him lose his appetite and lay awake in bed at night.

"How else should she be?" Archie asked, cocking his head at Rupert as though he were puzzled. Rupert shook his head, trying to clear the anger and the port-fog, since he'd been drinking for many hours already today. He had to focus on this conversation.

"We had a slight misunderstanding last week, and I thought she might be upset with me," Rupert admitted reluctantly. Was he ready to talk about what had happened between him and Lizzie? Seeing the knowing look on Archie's face, it seemed his hand was being forced.

"I didn't realise she was your latest mistress," Archie said casually, flicking a piece of invisible lint off his jacket.

Rupert clenched his teeth against the overwhelming feeling to smash his fist into something.

"She isn't." Lizzie had never been his mistress. His lover maybe, but never his mistress. The word was too common. She wasn't common, and what Rupert felt for her wasn't common.

"So, you aren't bedding her?" Archie asked lightly.

"I was," Rupert admitted darkly. He hated the admission being phrased as though it was past tense. She wasn't in the past for him, and after he had all but forced her to refuse Viscount Courtney's proposal, he hoped he wasn't in her past either.

"So, you've found someone to replace her?" Archie asked, a small amount of interest entering his voice.

Rupert shook his head.

"Rupert, I owe you, more than I can say, for standing by me after my brother's death, so I have brought news for you. Lizzie was planning on going back to her estate for the rest of the Season, but I believe Charlotte has talked her out of it."

Rupert was still lost. He clenched his massive fists and loosened them gradually, taking in a deep breath. How could that be?

"Why would she leave?" he asked quietly, staring at the table on which now stood an empty bottle of port. Had he drunk all of that?

"I believe she is worried that you will flaunt your latest conquest in front of her," Archie answered, waving his hand as though it were obvious.

"I wouldn't do that," Rupert said quickly. "And why would she think such a thing?" he said quietly, mostly to himself. Had he hurt her that much by breaking off contact between them? He hadn't meant to damage their relationship. He just needed time to think.

"She believes that she did something to upset you, not the other way around."

Rupert swallowed painfully, speechless for the first time in his life. He had to know more.

"Did she tell you why?" he whispered.

Archie nodded and Rupert, who had never backed down from a fight before, dropped his head and refused to make eye contact with his friend.

How horrific. Could Lizzie have revealed what had passed between them?

"What did she tell you?" he croaked, and then roughly cleared his throat. He couldn't seem to raise his head. How was he ever going to look at Archie again?

Archie set his glass down on the table with a clunk.

"She told us that she cares about you and doesn't want anyone else."

Rupert swallowed another lump that had lodged in his throat and tried to speak. Nothing came out. He placed his hand on his stomach to try to calm the unsettled feeling there. He tried again. "I think I've messed everything up, Archie," he admitted, the weight of his guilt terrifyingly massive.

"I thought I had too, and look where I am now," Archie reminded him.

Rupert couldn't help smiling at the memory of Archie lying unconscious, his head in Charlotte's lap. No one had known what had been going on between them until Charlotte had announced her pregnancy. At that moment Archie's future had seemed very precarious.

"So, what do I do?" Rupert asked, lifting his heavy gaze to his friend.

"Do you want to marry her?"

"I don't know," Rupert answered honestly. The idea was foreign. When he was younger, he had believed he would never marry. Then when he found out he had to, he had thought he would have a modern *ton* marriage. A marriage in which he would continue his discreet affairs and she could have hers. He had never assumed he would find a woman he *wanted* to marry.

Archie made an impatient noise and pushed himself back in his chair. "Bollocks."

"Pardon?" Rupert asked, blinking at the cuss word coming out of his perfect friend's mouth.

"You heard me. It's quite simple. She loves you, and you care about her. You must marry for your brother's sake at some point, and she wants a family. What's stopping you? It appears to be a simple solution."

Rupert blinked at how easy Archie made everything seem.

"I never really thought to marry," he admitted honestly. His parents had a horrible marriage where they had different lives, and his brother's marriage, which had started out so different, was now worse than that of his parents.

"Look, Rupert, if all of us took our parents or siblings' marriages as examples, none of us would marry. But look at Oliver and me. We're making a success of ours," Archie crooned.

Rupert thought that was a slight understatement and grinned wryly. He released a huge sigh and let the words come that he had been locking in a box for weeks.

"And if I can't be faithful? Or she can't have children?" Rupert voiced his greatest fears. He did love Lizzie. But what would happen if he couldn't be faithful, or God forbid, she cuckolded him when he was still faithful to her?

Archie made another disgusted noise. "Do you want anyone else now?"

"No," Rupert admitted, embarrassed. He'd always had several interests at once. No one woman had ever held his attention for long. The fact that he admitted that Lizzie did spoke volumes.

"Then why do you assume that's going to change?" Archie demanded again.

He obviously wasn't going to let Rupert out of this dilemma easily.

"And as for having children, that is a gamble you take with any wife. You never wanted the title, so if it passes to a distant cousin, do you care?"

Rupert heard the words, but they took a while to sink in. Was that the problem? Was he so worried about failing as his brother had, that he would sacrifice being with the woman he loved?

A weight Rupert hadn't been aware he had been carrying, shifted. As though shackles had been unlocked, Rupert's entire body became lighter, happier. Why did his life have to end because of a promise he had made seven years ago? If he married a woman he loved, his life would only get better, not worse.

"You're right," Rupert said slowly, as though the idea hadn't quite cemented in his mind yet. What was he waiting for? An archangel to come down from heaven and hit him on the head? Lizzie wanted him, and Rupert loved her, so why was he sitting here wasting time?

He stood up abruptly, swaying from fatigue and port.

Archie laughed, grabbed Rupert's forearm and tugged him back into his seat.

"I think you need a coffee, then you can see her."

Archie smiled openly at Rupert, and for the first time, Rupert was struck by how truly happy Archie was. They, as a group, hadn't realised the weight and responsibility Archie had always hidden behind his polish and social armour. With the weight lifted, he looked younger and indeed more handsome.

Rupert obligingly drank the coffee that was put in front of him, and even ate the steak they served him. He was impatient to get to Lizzie, but talking to a woman you had grievously injured required one's full attention. There was a possibility that there would be some grovelling involved.

Chapter 15

Half an hour later they were on Archie's front step.

"Just remember to tell her the truth," Archie advised before they reached the front knocker.

"Pardon?" Rupert almost shouted in panic, pulling Archie back a step.

"I know you would prefer just to propose and get on with it, but she won't want that. She'll want a full explanation, and she may not forgive you straight away."

Rupert stood dumbstruck. Was Archie serious? He had thought just to apologise, propose and get her into bed as quickly as possible. Wasn't that how it was going to happen?

"Did you have to explain everything?" he asked, suspicious.

Archie flushed lightly, his usually pale complexion pinkening.

"Yes, but after the wedding. I was lucky," he said with a rather wolf-like smile. "She had to marry me."

And with those words ringing in his ears, Rupert followed Archie into his townhouse.

"Does my wife still have her guest with her?" Archie asked the butler.

"Yes, my lord. They are in the dining room, sitting down to a light luncheon. Shall I tell the housekeeper to set two more places?"

"That would be wonderful," Archie replied without even glancing at Rupert, and again Rupert found himself being dragged along behind his friend.

A waiting footman opened the dining room door, and Rupert was thankful that, being Archie's home, they wouldn't need to be introduced.

"Hello again, Lizzie," Archie greeted Lizzie as he walked up to the end of the table where the ladies sat.

"Just set two more places here," Archie motioned to the footman who had moved to the opposite end of the table.

Charlotte smiled at her husband and held out her hand.

"I didn't realise you had gone out, my dear." Her eyes twinkled.

Archie bowed and kissed her hand. "I went to the club and was lucky enough to find Rupert there."

Rupert couldn't pull his eyes away from where Lizzie sat opposite Charlotte, looking pale and so beautiful. He had known how much he loved her, but he had forgotten how the very sight of her stopped the air in his lungs and made his body quicken.

* * *

Lizzie looked down into her soup and clenched her jaw tightly, tingles crawling up her spine. She had no wish to see him. Why had she not run away without telling anyone?

Archie indicated which seat Rupert should take, which was opposite Lizzie and next to Charlotte.

He bowed to his hostess. "Charlotte," he greeted her, kissing her hand.

"How is my future godchild this day?" He reached out rather slowly and gently lay his hand on Charlotte's large belly.

Lizzie choked on her tears as she watched Rupert reverently caress Charlotte's still-growing child. How often had she dreamed of carrying a baby? She had never thought Rupert would be a man to touch another man's pregnant wife in such a way.

Lizzie could feel a sob rising in her pained throat and then the words registered as though they were being spelled out for her slowly.

"Godchild?" she questioned, noting the tears in Charlotte's eyes as well. Perhaps it wasn't a standard gesture for Rupert to make?

"Good afternoon, my lady," Rupert greeted her politely, bowing, but not making his way around the table to touch her.

"About two months ago Charlotte informed me that I was going to be the godfather to their next child. I was honoured to be told I was their choice."

He gave her a smile that told her how happy he had been that day, but there was something else in his face. He looked calm, more so than she had ever seen him.

"Sit down, Rupert, and dine with us," Charlotte invited cheerily.

"Thank you," he returned, sitting down.

"How is little John?" Rupert asked politely, enquiring about

Charlotte and Archie's son. He was just over a year old and quite a little devil.

Charlotte laughed happily and began regaling him with tails of her offspring's first words and the like. Lizzie's head was spinning, and anger as well as guilt swirled in her like a stormy sea.

Why was everyone acting like this was an everyday occasion? Didn't they know how uncomfortable she was? How much did she not want to be here?

"Should I ask for some lunch for you, Rupert? Have you eaten?" Charlotte asked, apparently concerned.

"Archie and I ate at our club, thank you," he murmured.

Lizzie looked at him and noticed dark smudges under his eyes. Perhaps he hadn't been eating properly? When he caught her eye, he smiled at her, and she dropped her gaze to her plate, stabbing at the apple tart with her fork.

Rupert reached for a glass of water, and Lizzie stared, sharing a concerned look with Charlotte. What was wrong with him?

"Yes?" he asked.

Charlotte just smiled, but Lizzie couldn't hold in the words.

"Why are you drinking water? Are you ill?" she asked, genuinely concerned. Did he have a fever? She began to stand up to check, but his chuckle made her sit down again.

"I just thought it was a good time to start looking after myself, is all." He laughed again and asked for more water.

"Any particular reason?" Charlotte asked, her eyes falsely innocent.

"Yes. It's time to marry, I believe, and no lady wants to marry a drunkard, does she?" Rupert asked rather rhetorically. He took another sip of his water.

"Have you chosen the lucky lady?" Charlotte asked, grinning despite her best efforts.

Rupert nodded. "I have. I just have to ask."

"You're getting married?" Lizzie asked, dumbstruck. Could Rupert be so cruel as to come here and rub her nose in the fact that he had found the person he wanted to share his life with? He couldn't seem to spend a moment with her without losing his sanity, yet not even a week later he had found the woman to whom he would be tied eternally.

"Hopefully, I…"

Lizzie ran. She picked up her skirts and fled from the dining room. Her heart was pounding, and her hands were shaking, but she needed to get away from these terrible people, now. How could they not care at all for her feelings?

She made it to the front door and reached to collect her coat and bonnet, ready to make a mad dash into the street.

Rupert came charging down the hallway like a bull, and she squealed. He hefted her up onto his shoulder, and she beat her fists on his back and shrieked as loudly as she could.

How dare he handle her like some errant child?

He ignored her feeble attempts to free herself and turned to address the butler who had rushed into the entrance area at the ruckus.

"Mrs. Symmons and I need to talk privately about a misunderstanding. Is there somewhere we can have that conversation?"

Lizzie hit Rupert's massive back again and attempted to get away. But he was too big, too strong, and her body was simply in too awkward a position.

Rupert started moving, walked into a room, shut the door, locked it and put the key in his pocket. Only then did he place Lizzie carefully down into a chair.

Lizzie put a hand to her pounding, spinning head. How dare he announce he was getting married and then prevent her from leaving? What did he want? One last tumble before he was tied for life to another woman?

"What the hell do you think you are doing?" Lizzie exploded, her need to scream again gathering in her overheated body. She pushed herself to her feet, needing to kick, punch, yell.

Rupert fell to his knees in the middle of the sitting room.

Lizzie froze. The heat leached from her face, but she remained standing. Her angry words stuck in her throat. Rupert was on his knees, in the middle of the day, looking at her like she was the sun and the moon combined.

"What are you doing?" she asked, rather obtusely.

"I'm proposing marriage to the woman I love," he announced, all the love that Lizzie had hoped to see in his eyes, shining back at her.

Her knees sagged, and she fell back into the chair behind her. Was he serious? When had he changed his mind? When had he realised this?

"When did you figure out that you loved me?" Lizzie asked, dazed.

Rupert swallowed visibly. "I realised it when we made love on the piano," he told her, refusing to get up from his knees until she gave him an answer.

"But...you left me!" she all but screamed at him. Why was the man so confusing?

"I know. I was terrified of what it meant. But I've come to apologise and tell you the truth. I didn't think falling in love would happen to me. But it has, and I'm hoping that you will make me the happiest of men by consenting to sleep next to me for the rest of my life."

Lizzie blinked like an owl. Did The Honourable Rupert

Willoughby just declare love and an intention of fidelity? Impossible!

"You won't have any other women?" Lizzie asked doubtfully.

"No, I won't. If you promise not to consort with anyone else, either."

Lizzie choked on a laugh. Her? Cuckold him? "Why would I go to anyone else when you're all I want?" She sighed.

Rupert's face lit up like a yule log. "So, you'll marry me?"

Lizzie chewed on her lip. Of course, she was going to marry him, but she needed to establish a few things first.

"Where would we live?" she asked, cocking her head.

She had never disclosed to him how much money she had. Few people knew, even if he had bothered to ask around.

"Wherever you like. I currently live in my bachelor townhouse, but I also have a small country estate if that is where you would prefer to be. I also have a rather good income due to Archie's advice on investing. I am my brother's heir, so although I couldn't afford to buy us a townhouse initially, we won't lack any other comforts."

Lizzie smiled at Rupert's attempts to reassure her. He wasn't used to talking about his assets, that was quite evident.

"Children?" Lizzie asked, crossing her arms. She had been overwhelmed when she had seen him touch Charlotte's pregnant belly, but it gave her hope that he would someday look at her like that.

Rupert swallowed.

"I want children," he whispered. "With you."

"Girl children?" Lizzie couldn't help asking. He would be under a lot of pressure to produce an heir. Would their marriage go the same way that his brother's had if they couldn't beget a son?

"Any sort that comes our way. I never really cared about the title, so if it passes to my cousin, then that is the way it is supposed to be," he declared.

"Oh, what if I can't," Lizzie cried helplessly, letting her hands fall into her lap. Here she was, making Rupert earn her trust and respect, and yet she was the one with the fear of being found unsatisfactory.

Rupert dragged himself up onto the chair next to her and gently pulled her into his lap. Lizzie went into his arms gladly, settling into his lap with a sigh and burrowing into his shoulder.

"Whatever happens, happens, Lizzie. I just want *you*."

Lizzie sobbed against his shirt, the stress from the past few weeks welling up inside her and breaking forth, like the pressure of water breaking free.

"I just want you too," she sobbed happily, tilting her head up for a kiss.

His big hand came around her chin and pulled her face up to his.

"Then you'll marry me?" he said, uncertainty still swirling around those amazing blue eyes.

Lizzie laughed and wrapped her arms around his neck.

"Of course, I'll marry you, I love you too." And with that declaration, Rupert kissed her and kept kissing her, and would continue all the days of their lives.

Epilogue

Lizzie had been wrong about one thing. The happiest day of her life arrived two years after their wedding day. It had taken her more than a year to conceive, and when she finally did, she had been so worried for her baby she had hardly moved from her bed. It was only the assurances of both Charlotte and Sarah that had gotten her up and moving again.

She had been afraid to let her rather large husband into her body too, and he had been remarkably understanding about her fears. Both Sarah and Charlotte had been pregnant with their third babies around the same time, and they both professed not to be able to get enough of their husbands.

Lizzie had decided to try and found that her body was the same. Her touch also gave Rupert the intimacy he needed, for she had found that since their wedding day he did not sleep without her. Even through those weeks of her flux and choice of abstinence, he would hold her all night.

And now, almost two years to the day since she had married her handsome, blue-eyed man, she had given birth to his son. A replica of Rupert, he had black hair, blue eyes and the most gorgeous face Lizzie had ever seen.

Rupert had been there for the actual delivery, which had been most unorthodox. As was customary, he had been sent from the bedroom when the pains had started. But after more than twenty-four hours in labour and when the pains had gotten so fast and so intense that Lizzie couldn't help screaming out, Rupert had burst in to support her. He had voiced concerns early in her pregnancy that she would not beear a baby with his height well and he had been terrified that she would die and leave him. He had held her hand, mopped her brow and promptly burst into tears when his son had been laid upon Lizzie's breast.

The birth had been difficult, but the doctor assured them that it had all been perfectly normal for a first baby.

"He is perfect," Rupert cooed at his son.

Lizzie lay against the pillows. The maids had come and helped her while Rupert had held their baby. She was now clean, bathed and exhausted. While she'd been attended to, Rupert had taken the baby's swaddling off and laid him out on a blanket, naked. He was perfect. Long and thin, Lizzie was sure he would fill out like his father in no time.

"You're happy we had a boy?" Lizzie asked, elated despite her determination not to care about the sex.

Rupert looked at her and gave her a smile so sweet that her heart melted all over again.

"I am, but when he was laid on your chest, I didn't even know what he was. I just knew that we had a baby and you were still here with me. Nothing else mattered."

The tears welled up, and she let them, happier than she ever had been.

"Thank you so much for loving me," Lizzie whispered through her tears.

"No, thank you for never giving up on me," Rupert said fiercely, cupping her face and bringing her lips up to his for a perfect kiss.

"So, six weeks 'til I get you to myself again?" Rupert asked, not sounding entirely disappointed by this.

Lizzie nodded, weary and sublimely happy. Slowly, with her husband and child by her side, she drifted into sleep.

Rupert stayed watching his wife for a long time after she fell asleep. He sat in the chair next to her bed with his newborn son in his arms and gave thanks for all of his blessings.

He had finally found the woman who was his other half, his equal, his *better*. She loved him unreservedly and had total faith in their marriage. That, in turn, left him feeling confident and loved. He had been jealous, initially, of any men who danced with her or tried to get her alone. But she had proven to be unstintingly loyal, and he had been the same.

He often laughed with Archie about the fact that he had once been worried that he couldn't stay faithful to one woman. Lizzie fulfilled every fantasy he ever had in the bedchamber. And when she hadn't been able to give him that during part of her confinement, the comfort of her warmth and presence in his bed was enough to keep him satisfied.

And he now had a son. The next heir to the Earl of Sweeting. Rupert's mouth curled into a wry smile. His father would have been proud. His brother would be elated. It was bittersweet. He wanted a son for his sake, not just as the heir to a fortune and title.

He looked down at his son and smiled again.

"We'll just have to make sure we take after Archie and Oliver, my boy. Lots of brothers and sisters for you."

He looked down on Lizzie's sleeping form, taking in her larger breasts and beautiful skin. His cock stirred, and he sighed. He would always want this woman, no matter what she looked like or what they had gone through.

She was his, and he was hers, through and through.

Rupert rocked his son to sleep, still chuckling gently. He would give Lizzie the large family she wanted, and he knew in doing so, he had found his purpose in life.

THE END

* * *

Download book 4 now:
https://books2read.com/u/medBxY

Or read on for a sneak peek into the next story in 'The Heir and the Spare' series.

Hannah's Rakehell Duke

* * *

Chapter 1

Lord John Dunford, second son of the Duke of Arrow, swallowed down the vomit that rose in his throat. His sister and her husband were truly nauseating. They stroked each other constantly and made eyes at one another across the table at every meal. He'd never seen the like of it before. And to think that Archie had once upon a time been his best friend.

"So, who is the young lady you have visiting with you, Charlotte?" John asked, demanding attention from the besotted pair.

Charlotte and Archie finally looked away from each other to address him.

"My cousin. She arrived late yesterday," Archie murmured, idly stroking Charlotte on the back of the neck with his fingers.

John glared at the man that he used to consider one of his best friends. There was a time and a place for such affection, and it was not at the dining table.

Archie cleared his throat and dropped his hand away.

"Really, John," Charlotte snapped, her eyes flashing dangerously. "If you don't like how we are with each other, you can go back to London and the boredom that comes with it."

John ignored her, shifting in his chair. He had nowhere else to go and she knew it.

"Tell me about your cousin, Archie."

Surely there would be something to amuse him while visiting his sister.

"Hannah," Archie said, a winsome smile stretching across his usually solemn face.

Worried about his sister's feelings, John's eyes darted across to Charlotte to find the same look on her face.

How odd.

"Hannah is, well..." Archie twisted his wrist in the air as though searching for the right word to describe his cousin.

"American," Charlotte finished for her husband.

"Really? Well, then I am intrigued." He'd never met an American woman before and he had heard they were indeed an unusual breed.

"Is she a widow?" John asked. Hoping, of course, that she was. Perhaps Hannah was the perfect something that would take his mind off the fact that his life was in shambles.

His three best friends had all married themselves off and he had been left standing alone. Not only had they gotten leg-shackled—that would have been tolerable—but they had all made love matches. They had stopped drinking, carousing, and were generally so smitten it was sickening to be around them.

Even Rupert, a man who'd drunk his way through every brothel in London, was now sick in love.

To make matters even worse, John had nowhere else to go in the off Season. He'd spent his adult years visiting his friends because the family estate in Hampshire was too awkward and uncomfortable to visit. His mother became more and more distressed every year about the long-term presence of his father's mistress. Due to this discord, his father spent more and more time with his mistress. It was not a pleasant situation.

Archie had his family's spectacular family home in Kent and John had always been welcome, for which he was grateful. But John could barely tolerate Archie and Charlotte's company now, which was bad luck for him because he was out of choices. Oliver and Sarah were at their own grand country estate with their two sons, and Rupert had taken his beautiful new wife to France.

"Hannah is unmarried currently, looking for a husband this Season. Her father, a distant cousin of mine, contacted me last year and I offered to sponsor her." Archie said, giving John a meaningful stare.

Damn. A virgin? He wasn't going near her then.

John laughed, letting some of his built-up tension free. If his friend thought he would be married off anytime soon, then Archie was setting himself up to be sorely disappointed.

"I'm glad I can meet her first then, Archie. I can warn her of the dangerous rake hells that scour London."

John chuckled again as he watched unease flicker over his friend's face. What in the hell was he going to do with a virgin, other than flirt with her to annoy Archie?

"I think that would be a great idea," Charlotte said as she placed her hands in her lap. "She should be back in the stable by now. Go introduce yourself, brother."

Archie smiled, the light in his eyes a little too mischievous for John's liking.

"Why would she be in the stables?" John asked in confusion.

No lady was ever found in a stable.

"She'll be attending to her horse, I'm sure."

"She rides?" John asked, unable to quell the slight interest that pricked his voice. Although it wasn't totally unheard of, a lady who rode was rare, although Lizzie, Rupert's wife, certainly did. Perhaps Hannah was a country girl also and they could share their passion for good horse flesh. Maybe she wouldn't be such a loss after all.

"Mm," Archie murmured, nodding his head, and putting his arm back around his wife's chair.

That decided it for him. He wasn't staying here a moment longer to watch any more of the wonderful show titled, 'My sister and her sap of a husband'.

"Then I shall introduce myself." John stood up and bowed to his family. Although he was using the woman as an excuse in a way, he was interested in meeting a new member of the female species. An American lady who rode horses? He thought he had bedded every sort there was available, but this was new.

John trotted off toward the stables, fresh air filling his lungs. His heart felt lighter from being outdoors. He tilted his head towards the sun and glanced across at the large green field behind the house. Once upon a time, Archie and he used to talk about nothing but horses. Now all of Archie's conversations revolved around his sons, his wife, and his estate. John was bored with it all.

John rounded the stable door and stopped dead in his tracks. He couldn't be looking at a woman, surely? The person before him looked like a well-dressed stable hand.

Could this really be the American cousin, Hannah?

She was rubbing down a magnificent horse with the exuberance of a seasoned stable hand. She had a thick bristled brush and she was working her way across the animal's hide, making gentle chatter to the horse.

He watched a moment longer. The graceful arm movements, the hint of lush skin and shapely thigh. His body stirred. Yes, definitely a woman.

He held his breath as he moved closer. Hannah had long red-gold hair that fell down her back unbound and she wore male riding pants and a shirt. Looking closer John realized that the riding habit must be hers; no pair of pants designed for a man would ever fit a behind like that. It was so well-shaped he wanted to reach out and squeeze it.

Reminding himself that he was staring at a virgin who wanted to marry soon, John closed the gap between them.

He cleared his throat loudly to get her attention, but she just kept on brushing.

John bowed deeply and said in a loud voice, "John Dunford, your servant."

The lady in front of him jumped and whirled around laughing, sunshine lighting up the air around her like she was an angel in disguise.

"Charlotte's rapscallion of a brother? Good to meet you. I'm Hannah."

The woman with bright blue eyes and a brilliant smile stuck her hand out for him to shake.

John stared at her for a moment before good manners forced

him to shake the offered hand. He had gloves on and she did not, and he found himself wishing he hadn't dressed so formally today. He was flabbergasted. Dumbstruck.

Hannah was the most beautiful creature he had ever seen. More beautiful than Sarah, Lizzie, and Charlotte combined. And that was saying something because he admired all of his friend's wives.

She was covered in dirt, her hair was windblown, and yet she glowed with good health and a sensual promise that he'd be a fool not to recognise. Her cheekbones spoke of her aristocratic breeding and her full lips would make any woman envious.

An uncomfortable sensation twisted deep in his guts. He was confused as to how to act; what to do. He barely knew her and yet she was so different to any other woman he'd ever met.

The questions came shooting through John's head.

Why did she shake my hand like a man would?

Why is she here grooming the horses?

Why is she wearing men's trousers and not skirts?

Why is she looking at me with her clear blue eyes without a hint of fear, arousal, or disdain?

What's wrong with her?

"Hannah," he repeated slowly.

"Can I help you, John?" the beautiful, dirty woman asked, moving to the other side of the horse.

John watched her sure, strong hands working the brush and knew that this was not a new occupation for her. She had obviously spent most of her life doing that same action. What lady did that?

Pull yourself together, man.

"I was told by my sister to introduce myself." John smiled as he spoke, finally able to call on the easy charm that he usually possessed.

"Charlotte is a bit of a stickler for the rules, isn't she?" Hannah chortled again, and John put out his hand to steady himself. Good God. Had his knees weakened at the sound of her laugh?

"She is," John agreed, wondering for a moment if he had just insulted his sister. A smile quirked up one side of his mouth. This was delicious.

"Are you here for long, Hannah?"

John reached up to loosen his cravat, throwing caution to the wind. If she could dress in riding breeches, he could at least loosen the necktie threatening to choke him.

Why was there suddenly not a breath of fresh air around?

"Oh, most likely. My parents sent me over here to marry an Englishman. Quite given up on me, they have," Hannah confided in John without looking up from her work.

"Why would they despair of such a thing?" John asked incredulously. She was spectacular to look at and seemed to have an easy and happy disposition. Why would anyone despair of her marrying?

"I'm five and twenty." Hannah shrugged with indifference.

"No," John breathed, unable to believe she was any older than one and twenty. Her skin had a glow of youth most *ton* ladies lost at sixteen.

Hannah looked up, saw his expression, and burst out laughing.

John flushed. Why was she laughing at him? He clenched his teeth and crossed his arms across his chest.

He was six foot two inches and by no means thin. He worked hard to keep the muscle he had and yet at this moment, Hannah made him feel small and inadequate. Not a feeling he liked, nor one he was used to.

Hannah straightened from her hunched posture and cocked

her head to the side again while she gazed at him. She was much taller than most women John knew, easily five foot ten inches. It was a rare sight to be able to look in a woman's eyes so easily.

"Are you stuck up, too?" Hannah asked as she put the brush down. She came around the front of the horse and stood in front of him, placing her hands on her hips like a queen.

John couldn't stop his eyes travelling down her body.

Archie's cousin had wide hips and strong, nicely curved thighs. Thighs that could ride him for hours.

John's traitorous body rose at that thought.

"Are you quite finished looking me over?" Hannah demanded, flicking her long hair back over her shoulders.

John exhaled sharply as he saw the flush of her cheeks and the dangerous glitter in her oceanic eyes. She was spectacular when angry.

"Well, you do make a fetching picture, my lady," John drawled, stepping closer to pick up Hannah's hand.

She shook him off and placed her other hand square in the center of his chest.

"Back off," she said through clenched teeth.

"Pardon me?" John asked, his eyebrows shooting up his forehead. What on earth did she mean by that?

Hannah didn't repeat what she had said. Instead she shoved him backwards with one strong push of her hand.

John stumbled two steps back, a strange gargled laugh rolling out of his throat as he did. He hadn't been expecting it, and he would never have assumed a woman would do such a thing.

"I don't appreciate false compliments and I don't like charming dandies. So, I suggest you get used to a woman in trousers and I will see you at dinner."

John rubbed his chest where he had been pushed and enjoyed the sight of Hannah storming off toward the house, her arms swinging angrily, her beautiful thick hair moving around her like a cloud.

His eyes drifted lower and lust kicked him in the gut like a solid horse hoof.

She really must get a coat that covers that bottom of hers, he thought idly as he walked around the stables. What sort of lady was immune to his charms, was still unmarried at twenty-five, and was so spectacular looking?

John grinned happily. Perhaps the off Season wasn't going to be so dull, after all? At the very least, he didn't feel sorry for himself anymore.

At dinner, Hannah was even more beautiful than John had feared. He had hoped that cleaning her up might diminish her quality a little. Instead, it was like a penny that he had found in the dirt had been washed and polished, and turned out to be a golden sovereign.

"Your hair really is spectacular, Hannah," Charlotte sighed in awe.

Hannah chuckled good-naturedly and John's stomach tightened in a feeling he was beginning to identify as being solely related to the American. "That silly maid of mine tried to put it all up. It hurt my head. I will never understand how you do your hair like that every day."

Charlotte put her hand up to her beautifully coiffed hair and sighed.

"I had headaches for years when I was younger, but you get used to it."

John was surprised. How did he not know that?

"At least corsets are no longer in fashion." Charlotte giggled, her full breasts heaving over her dress. John looked away from his sister.

"One of the many reasons I am grateful to live today and not thirty years ago." Hannah smiled at Charlotte and took a long sip of her red wine. "I do like this wine, though a good whiskey is really my drink of choice."

John spat his wine out all over his empty plate.

He coughed, then pounded himself on the chest to clear his airways. Did she drink whiskey? What sort of lady drank whiskey?

"Are you all right, John?" Archie asked mildly, not commenting on the mess that now splattered his dining table.

"I apologize," John said hurriedly, leaning back so that the servants could clear away everything in front of him and lay out new cutlery, plates, and glasses.

Charlotte had a napkin covering her mouth and Hannah was glaring at him with an undue amount of anger.

John shrugged and tried to collect his dignity.

"What's wrong with whiskey?" Hannah asked, placing her glass of wine down with a thud.

John smiled and picked up his own glass of wine. He swallowed it without tasting it and smiled again at the beautiful enigma before him.

"I have never known a lady who drank whiskey."

Except a madam of a brothel maybe...

Hannah frowned and looked across at her cousin with a quizzical look on her face.

Archie inclined his head. "It is not common here, Hannah, that is true."

"Well, I shall not be changing myself for anyone." Hannah shrugged, calling to one of the footmen.

"Excuse me, what is your name?"

"Robbie, my lady." The young footman flushed and bowed.

"I would like the whiskey tray now, please...if that is all right with you, Charlotte?"

Hannah glanced across the table at her new friend, anxiety showing on her features for the first time.

Charlotte smiled brightly. "Hannah, you may have anything in this house that you like."

John watched the play of emotions crossing the three faces at the table and for the first time in a long time was highly entertained. Charlotte was having a great time, Archie was amused but wary, and Hannah's jaw was set with determination.

The whiskey tray arrived and John held up his hand.

"One for me, also."

Hannah looked up in surprise. She turned to John and asked him, "Can you recommend one?"

There were three bottles on the silver tray.

John knew each by color and shape of the bottle and pointed to his favourite. "The smallest bottle is the best," he drawled.

John thought himself quite a connoisseur of whiskey. Archie may not drink much himself but thankfully, he kept a stocked home.

Hannah poured each of them a glass and John pushed back his chair to stand up. Instead of waiting for him to retrieve it himself, Hannah stood with his glass and walked around the table to him.

"Here you go," she murmured, putting the half-full glass in front of him.

John jumped to his feet by reflex. He didn't think he had ever remained sitting whilst a lady was standing.

Hannah stepped back and laughed. "Oh, sit down," she swatted at him, hitting his arm in an attempt to encourage him to sit.

She moved back to her chair and John sat down gratefully. What sort of woman was this? That was twice in the same afternoon that she had hit him like an errant schoolboy. And damn it all, he wanted more. A lot more.

* * *

Read on here:
https://books2read.com/u/medBxY